# Gotta Earn a Living

## LEFT BANK

### Number 4

Blue Heron Publishing, Inc.
Hillsboro, Oregon

# Gotta Earn a Living

## LEFT BANK

### Number 4

Blue Heron Publishing, Inc.
Hillsboro, Oregon

Editor: Linny Stovall

Associate Editor: Stephen J. Beard

Publisher: Dennis Stovall

Staff: Daniel Foulkes, Mary Jo Schimelpfenig, Jean Wakefield

Copyeditor: Mary Catherine Lamb

Advertising: John Johnson

Interior Design: Dennis Stovall

Cover Design: Marcia Barrentine

Cover Photo: Making doughnuts at Franz Bakery (Photo #006500), courtesy of Oregon Historical Society

Advisors: Ann Chandonnet, Madeline DeFrees, Katherine Dunn, Jim Hepworth, Ursula K. Le Guin, Lynda Sexson, J. T. Stewart, Alan Twigg, Lyle Weis, Shawn Wong

Editorial correspondence: Linny Stovall or Stephen Beard, *Left Bank*, Blue Heron Publishing, Inc., 24450 N.W. Hansen Road, Hillsboro, Oregon 97124. Submissions are welcome if accompanied by a stamped, self-addressed envelope. Otherwise they will not be returned. Authors must have a strong connection to the Pacific Northwest. Submissions are read two months before deadline. Editorial guidelines are available on request (include SASE).

*Left Bank* is a series of thematic collections published semiannually by Blue Heron Publishing, Inc., 24450 N.W. Hansen Road, Hillsboro, Oregon 97124. Single editions are $7.95US (plus $2 s&h). Subscriptions (two editions) are available for $14. *Left Bank* is distributed to the book trade and libraries in the United States by Consortium Book Sales and Distribution, 1045 Westgate Drive, Saint Paul, Minnesota 55114-1065.

Rights and permissions not noted in the text: A different version of "A Matter of Degrees" was first published in *The San Francisco Chronicle, Sunday Punch* magazine. Kate Braid's "'Girl' on the Crew" was originally published in *Covering Rough Ground*, copyright 1991, Polestar Book Publishers. "The Redemption of Nick Carriere" is from *Voyages: At Sea with Strangers* by Joan Skogan, copyright © 1992 by Joan Skogan, HarperCollins Publishers Ltd. "Saving the Family Photographs," from *Fruit Fields in my Blood, Okie Migrants in the West* by Toby F. Sonneman, photographs by Rick Steigmeyer, is reprinted by permission of the University of Idaho Press, Moscow, Idaho. © 1992 by Toby F. Sonneman and Rick Steigmeyer.

Publication of this edition is made possible in part by a grant from the Oregon Institute of Literary Arts.

**LEFT BANK** #4: Gotta Earn a Living.
First edition, June 1993
Copyright © 1993 by Blue Heron Publishing, Inc.

ISBN 0-936085-54-1
ISSN 1056-7429

# contents

# foreword

For those of us old enough to remember, there once was an era when Ozzie and Harriet values dominated the culture and Dad could earn enough to support a family working just forty hours a week — even if the evidence of TV showed that breadwinner Ozzie Nelson never went to work, and that this did not seem to matter when homemaker Harriet shopped the neighborhood grocery.

Anyone who looks with nostalgia to the innocence and benignity of that time, however, needs to be reminded that it was also an era when people without regular employment were treated with contempt, when the roles men and women could play at work were restricted by cultural fiat, when the available jobs were labor-intensive, dirty, and even dangerous.

So in an era when Roseanne has apparently succeeded Ozzie Nelson as family icon, it may be appropriate to note that what has changed in the intervening years is almost everything — except the continuing need to earn one's living. This issue of *Left Bank* examines that need within the context of a changing culture, an uncertain economy, a rapidly evolving job market, and new perceptions about what the value of work ought to be.

Greg Bear opens the door with thoughts about the subversive nature of working without holding a job. David James Duncan, Tom Harpole, Kate Braid, and Richard Stine also share the convolutions and joy of chosen careers. Jeff Taylor, Toby Sonneman, and Joan Skogan honor or agonize over jobs they've left behind. Portraying the chilling hazards of work are Norman Maclean, Robin Cody, Sherman Alexie, Robert Heilman, and Kyle Walker. The absence of work lurks in pieces by Teri Zipf in her satire on a divorce; Sibyl James, whose Tunisian students prefer strikes over studies; and John Strawn, who confronts himself through Chilean street musicians. And more: poetry from Tom Wayman, William Johnson, Clem Starck, and Kent Chadwick. James Barker exhibits the work of survival in his photographs of Yup'ik life, and Adrian Raeside and Richard Stine share their wicked cartoon wits.

Provocative propositions to the current conceptions of worklife are offered by Jack Saturday, who turns the work ethic on its head; Gary Snyder, who shapes a community of alternative work and environment; and Joe Dominguez and Vicki Robin who have detached themselves from the workhorse of consumption.

Forget Ozzie and Harriet. Forget Roseanne, as well. Icons and role models are never as vibrant as real people; it just seems that way from the nimbus of lights that surround them. Here's a take on reality. We corralled a patch of it with this edition, and hope you find it enlightening, not to mention entertaining.

— The Editors

# INTRODUCTION:
# working

obert Frost said, "Home is the place where, when you have to go there,/ They have to take you in." He was a poet but probably knew more about work than I do. Work is like home. If you have to go there, they have to take you in, otherwise it isn't work. It's unemployment.

I haven't *worked* in eighteen years. Work is what you do for other people who pay you to do things they don't want to do. I've often caught myself saying, when I tell people I'm a writer, "It beats working."

Working sounds more impressive than writing. Labor is dignity. Work is pride. The sweat of the brow, broad backs, teeth bared, the sledge ha.m.- mer raised, the road built, building lifted, hog slaughtered, crops brought in, the long slow evenings on the porch after the harvest, smelling like a dog in your overalls, sweat caked in your armpits. That's work. Work smells bad. Hauling in great slapping blue tuna with a line; hefting crab pots full of unhappy crustaceans onto a violently unsteady deck. Work makes you sick. Pulling loaves of bread by the dozens from brick ovens, pouring them into bins, at four in the morning. Work makes you hungry.

Work. Labor. Dignified and real.

What goes on in my head is less like what the baker does and more like what happens inside the bread when it rises. Secret, microscopic, si- lent. I put it onto a keyboard and it sits on a disk, patterns written yes no yes no in magnetic film. Even printed on paper, it isn't bread. It's yeast for another mind. The changed minds are my bread.

That sounds subversive. Good honest labor is not subversive; it is the turning of the screwdriver or the torquing of the wrench against nature, against matter; it is lifting matter and bending or smashing it to one's will. I bend words and ideas, tougher than steel. But that isn't work. I lift no weight.

**10** Sometimes it feels as if I'm involved in another kind of labor, as the novel emerges, a manuscript weighing eight pounds on paper, after a year's growth and forming. I sympathize with the pregnant mother-to-be, carrying this bulky infant within her; my head feels swollen, I don't listen too closely, I complain, I am always remaking some part, staring at a wall or sitting on a couch. That isn't work. But in that last sentence, before I changed it, *remaking* read *reworking*. The language is confused.

As in, *The Works of Shakespeare. The Complete Works of Beethoven.*

In the future, no one will *go to work*, we are told. We'll all stay home. That's more like what I do, which isn't work. If you can't go there, and they don't have to take you in, it isn't work. If you can't take a lunchpail and clock in, it probably isn't work, either.

In the future, robots (from the Czech word for worker) will do all our heavy work. Right now, *workers* are being put out of work by machines that resemble more and more the robots of old movies, but usually without legs or heads. Just arms. I would worry if I did a lot of *work* with just my arms. I use my arms, but I do not worry that a robot will take over my writing. I don't write turgid bestsellers; robots could do that, but not what I do. So writing turgid bestsellers is probably work.

But in the future, computers and neural-net thinkers and other wonderful machines will do a lot of things besides make cars. They'll control communications, banking, hotel reservations, hospital records; they'll become sophisticated at stock transactions, rather than buying or selling all at once like manic depressives. That will put lots of people out of work. What will these people do?

Some of us may believe it is fun to carry bricks and answer telephones. I don't. What I do isn't always *fun*, but it is essential. I can't imagine not doing it. If you can imagine not doing something, retiring or quitting or just getting away from it all, then that should be called work. I can imagine not carrying bricks.

Still, labor is dignified. It's had a lot of good press. I feel good after a day of clearing brush or cutting wood or moving furniture; sometimes sore muscles feel good. I imagine I'm in Chicago in the thirties wearing overalls, black stamped-tin lunchpail grasped in my WPA ham-sized fist, big Bluto arms straining at my rolled-up sleeves, going to work with my broad back to kill pigs or forge steel. I think *Carl Sandburg* or *John Steinbeck* or *Upton Sinclair* or *Frank Norris*. I hum Woody Guthrie songs.

Here's something that could really guarantee a steady income. Work, and then write about it. Do something that you can imagine not doing, that is unusual and difficult and dangerous, and quit and write about how awful and exciting it was. Robots won't be doing all of that for quite a while. Maybe they're too smart.

Here is what the future will be like. If you carry heavy things around, you are out of luck. A machine will carry heavy things. Maybe you'll get to fix the machine, until another machine can do that. (Watch out when machines start building and fixing machines. Evolution might sneak in somewhere.) If you think simple thoughts or perform simple organizing tasks, such as filing or bookkeeping or sorting letters, you'll be lucky to train the machine that replaces you.

But if you do things no machine has yet been able to do — besides walk without falling over — you'll probably have work in the future. You'll commute from your living room to your computer in the home office, probably on foot. You'll hook into WORKNET and poke around on electronic job boards for tasks that other people and machines do not want to do.

Make the most of it. Carry a lunchpail. Think of *Steinbeck*.

But blame Asimov and Heinlein and Clarke. It's science fiction writers who inspire people to build robots and automate.

Maybe in the future, nobody will *work* at all.

Maybe we'll all be writers.

I don't think that will work.

*Unidentified baker, Franz Bakery*

JEFF TAYLOR

# carnal knowledge

*Work is love made visible.*
— Kahlil Gibran

riters usually have spotty résumés. Scratch any of them deeply enough, and you'll find some horrible employments they've had to take to support their writing habit, or to gather material, or simply to keep eating. If you ask writers about their Worst Job, they'll be able to recall it instantly, using the index of lasting scars on their psyche.

But I submit that in any Worst Job contest among writers, I would win if the criteria were duration and vileness. To other writers, I must respectfully say: Screw your pathetic little entries, your tales of brief inconvenience and discomfiture. Never tell your leaky-rowboat stories to a survivor of the Titanic. Fourteen-hour days raking asphalt in the hot sun? Yes, I've done that too, for entire summers; it was like being a sex therapist in Aspen. Other writers may have worked in packing plants also; but I alone served the carnal gods inside the true Temple of Meat during its darkest historical hour, and I rotted therein for nine months, each second of which lasted several eternities.

Imagine my delight when my old employer made the news a few years ago. Federal investigators described the company as a corporate outlaw with connections to organized crime and meted out million-dollar fines for health and marketing violations. Prison sentences were even mentioned. The plant singled out as the hub of abuses, the Black Hole of a bad, bad industry, was my alma mater.

In 1974, needing big money to leave the Midwest, I worked in the largest beef-processing facility in the world. A mini-career in the field of commercial cattle mutilation is an experience not to be confused with fun. But I learned much about the resilience of the human spirit, made new friends as unfortunate as I, and gained a fresh perspective on cow meat. The universe does not contain enough catsup to drown those memories.

Picture a refrigerated concrete building the size of several football fields, where thousands toiled in a soul-sucking cold on brick floors that were always slippery with the grease of the bovine departed. Somewhere inside, yours truly contributed to the carnage.

**14**    Squatting nearby, eighteen years ago, was a city. I had lived in its churning bowels too long; let us call it Puke City, Iowa. Every morning at zero-dark-30, I exchanged a day of my life and most of my innocence for enough money to buy distance in perpetuity. In my humble opinion, this would be an excellent place to mothball nuclear devices. The worst that could happen is they'd all accidentally go off.

So much for the why; now we come to the *what*. The first hour of Day One, we trainees sat in a small room, watching an orientation movie of the company's new Learjet on takeoff: a smooth landing, industry executives deplaning and slithering into limousines in New Jersey, a few posed handshakes with donnish Mafioso types, and segue to takeoff again, but going the other way. Fade to the company logo, with fanfares and flourishes. "Any questions?" the orientation officer asked. Afterwards we descended to the company store, a cage with a cash register where we could buy white coats at cost.

In its benevolence, the company gave us hard hats, a glove made of steel mesh to protect the hand that held our very own meathook, a pair of foam earplugs, and a stern warning not to mitigate our daily horror with drugs. Now fully equipped, we took a tour of the plant, beginning with the department precisely called Slaughter.

There, in darkness visible, we saw our very first abominations. Most of what I remember is thoroughly unprintable, and I've repressed the really bad stuff except for occasional sweatmares. They made us an offer: dead-eyed zombies clad in rubber suits were paid a bonus of twenty-five cents per hour for wading up to their knees in lakes of blood. No takers? A few who wish to quit already? The rest of you come along then, and abandon all hope anyway.

The plant was divided into Outside Meat, where most of us would work, and Inside Meat, a land of organs, brains, guts, and whatnot, destined for frankfurter wienies. With its Acme Body Cavity Evacuators and steel bowls full of staring eyeballs, this last place was only slightly less obscene than Slaughter. Again, offers were made. Adamant refusals followed.

Thence to a giant refrigerator door, which opened into a purgatory of brilliant lights, in predominant colors of white, red-on-white, and chrome.

My new home, Outside Meat: pieces of cow muscle ran by on a hundred conveyors, countless people hacking at them with knives in a tornado of background roar. Hard to believe it was springtime outside. Or anywhere.

The remainder of our orientation was delivered in barely audible shouts. We were cautioned not to feed our hands into machinery, as one hapless worker had done recently. Now, they explained in screams, they had a thousand pounds of hamburger adulterated with three feet of right arm from fingernails to deodorant, unfit even for the military market. Not to mention an employee who could only be retrained to open limousine doors.

The first month, I chose a knifeless job, boxing meat at the end of a conveyor. Twenty-pound chunks of flesh kept coming at me from the endless belt, and empty boxes slid down a chute in the ceiling. Except when they didn't. If the box machine on the floor above broke down, meat had to be stacked on steel tables for later breakneck catching-up once the boxes resumed. This was considered a high-stress job, and they told me about the man I replaced. On the box machine's thousandth breakdown, he stopped working, letting an avalanche of meat spill on the floor beside him as he stared up the empty box chute. He tried to climb it, much like a child clambering up a playground slide except for the meathooks in both hands and the obscenities he was screaming. Plant security surrounded and Maced him before he could unravel anyone on the box crew, and he was hauled away for psychiatric observation.

This station soon lost its charm, and I transferred to the night shift to cut meat. Deboners made more money, and got to watch the belt move sideways instead of head-on. This may sound like a small thing, but it affected even my dreams, in which monsters, knives, and locomotives now moved past from left to right, instead of directly at me.

At first, the cold bothered me. But soon I understood how Tibetan monks can sit naked in blizzards and dry soggy sheets with their bodies. The trick is to ignore the physical body's pleas — *Oh, this is miserable, why the hell are we here?* — and just keep on transcending. To add to the surrealism, large plastic barrels marked "OM" were scattered everywhere in that section of the factory. In there, it stood only for Outside Meat.

Perhaps you wonder about abscesses, a buzzword in the federal hearings. Unless you are a vegetarian, you may not care to know that they are a cheerful yellow-green. Carnivores should skip this whole paragraph. FYI, an abscess is an infection in the meat, which pops under the knifepoint and contaminates everything for a cubic yard or so with — feel free to pass on this bit of upcoming information — organic chartreuse slime, flecked with bits of — never mind, the gorge rises even to recall it. Sorry I brought it up.

Proper procedure, although I never saw it happen, was to shut down the conveyor, notify the government inspector, and bring in live steam hoses to disinfect the entire line. Usually, meaning ten times out of ten, a foreman swabbed off most of the goo with a green rag, while the inspector magically vanished; according to the grapevine, he dropped by the bathroom to pick up an envelope containing a little token of management's esteem. The belt was not supposed to stop, *ever*, except to extricate the occasional human face or body part from the turning cogs.

To prevent complacency and increase profits, new outrages were introduced weekly: longer hours, faster lines, duller knives. United by our hatred for the work and our employer, a thousand weary voices raised a wail of bitching at these times, but the company's response (practically the corporate motto) was: "So quit." Turnover was fierce, and those who stayed had to find ways to temporarily shelve their sanity.

There was one fellow with the oddest kaleidoscopic eyes, whose entire job consisted of watching pelvic bones fall down into a giant hole at the end of the conveyor. Occasionally, he would grab an incoming bone and put it on a belt going in the opposite direction; someone had not cleaned every scrap of gristle from it.

It struck me as easy money until he invited me to look down into the pit. Fifty feet below, giant grinders chomped the bones to pulverized muck. The opening was large enough to accommodate an automobile, and the hypnotic roll of the grinders seemed to beckon; a person could just dive in and end it all. With an effort, I pulled myself back.

I asked him how he stood it. He thought and thought and thought, finally opening his mouth very wide, eyes squeezed shut. Moments passed. "Aaaaacid," he finally whispered at the top of his lungs; LSD in megadoses, every morning before work. "Did you know...mannnn...that the walls in this place...*breathe?*"

No, this had escaped my attention heretofore. But now I saw what he meant. In a way, the building was a giant organism. We had been swallowed by the system, like yogurt bacteria, for the purpose of breaking down cattle into digestible components. At times, the entire tableau seemed to freeze, and I saw myself as one tiny cell in the epithelium of some dark beast's stomach, flagellating my cilia like crazy to process cow flesh .... Forfuggenever. It would never end, as long as humans ate beef. I could never leave until the beast sloughed me off, or until I keeled over onto a conveyor belt and had the steaks cut away from my skeleton. Alternatively, I might throw myself down the cloaca of the Big Hole, to be ground into bone meal and dog food.

This depressing fantasy recurred every consecutive night for a week, the result of running out of pleasant things to think about. For any intellect higher than an earthworm's, the boredom was so vast that brain damage would have been welcome, and some actively courted it. One huge and hulking worker next to me ingested unknown chemicals from an eyedropper, taking them on his knees like a sacrament a few lockers away as the rest of us ate lunch. His mind was hamburger. From time to time, he'd tap me on the shoulder with his meathook point, silently holding up his razor-sharp boning knife like a psychotic mime: *Ready to die yet, guy?* Past caring, I'd shrug, glad for the diversion: *Feel free to kill me.* He'd shrug back, pull a slab of meat off the line, and slowly cut it to pieces.

My next job was cutting "shanks" off sides of beef, twelve per minute, leaving a certain portion of cow on the overhead hook and letting the "shank" thump down onto a conveyor. To save my life, I still could not find the "shank" on a live animal today; perhaps it has something to do with the shoulder. Across the conveyor alley were the bandsaws, whose operators dared not sneeze. (By contrast, we shankers could sneeze on the meat all we wanted, a precious freedom.) It required quantum levels of concentration to shove beef quarters into a bandsaw blade at the rate of 400 an hour. Eventually, I learned some of their names: Lupe, Mateo, Enriquito, Miguel, and Carmelo. To scare the shankers, sometimes they would close their eyes and go on pushing meat into the blade, until we begged them to look: *Sí, es muy macho, pero ¡Mira!* you stupid *cabrón.*

The job had consolations. I was able to meet people from every conceivable walk of life: students, farmers, Mexicans brought up in buses to break a strike who had stayed on and joined the union, doctoral candidates writing theses on workplace stress, communist agitators, housewives, the terminally confused, career criminals on sabbatical, and misfits of all description.

One night, a woman working next to me asked if I'd like to see a lion. Wondering what the hell, I said that would be fine.

After work, we went out to her car. On the front seat beside her husband was a purring lion cub, weighing only eighty pounds. I got to pick him up and stroke him, his fur rough as a terrier's, and he licked my face with a sandpaper tongue. They owned several cheetahs and jaguars, and this little lion was their newest family member. For five seconds, I wondered how they could feed that many big cats.

Thereafter, I looked at various pieces of meat going by on the belt with a new sense of wonder. Who would eat it?

A family with heads bowed, some dogface Army dragoon at Fort Remf, or perhaps a hungry lion in a barn down the road?

There is nothing like the smell of blood for arousing the herd instinct. We began to agree on collective definitions of reality, some of which approached mass hysteria. On hot full-moon nights, sudden fevers swept the plant like a pheromone wind; vans began rocking five minutes after quitting time, as workers paired off to explore the baser instincts with someone else's mate. I myself required no further carnal stimulation after eight solid hours of slapping meat. Strange flesh and moonlit sex orgies had a certain appeal, but my existence was already abundantly strange.

We also had spontaneous group sing-alongs. Now remember, a full shout barely carried six feet; obviously, there were no radios. But a catchy song that began on the lips of one worker would spread throughout the plant, just like in the movies, until it seemed that everyone was silently mouthing "The Mighty Quinn" or "Help Me, Rhonda," all of us thumping our knife handles on the conveyor when the chorus came up. Had the machinery suddenly stopped, it would have sounded like choirs of the damned; and over the thunder of machinery, the faintest ghost of the song must have percolated up to the higher reaches of management in a kind of aural contagion. The line bosses would return from the main office in a separate building to tell us the Gray Suits were humming what we were singing. There was no way they could have heard us.

Speaking of evil, drug use was pandemic. On the lunch hour, it was fashionable to go out to the cars for "buzz break," viz., dope smoking, although the attraction of an alkaloid that reputedly makes time crawl escaped me. To deal with drugs, the company invited federal and local agencies to halt consumption of any illegal substance that slowed production. (Cocaine was virtually unknown in those days, but employees who worked faster, for whatever reason, were given special consideration. Further affiant sayeth not.) When employees lit up in the parking lot, undercover agents would pull them from their cars and slam their faces into the asphalt at gunpoint. As part of the program, these wretches were then fired and cast into outer lightness to be prosecuted.

Such a determination to eradicate pot in the workplace would have been admirable, were it not for the acre of marijuana forest, virtual trees twelve feet tall that flourished in full view behind the plant during the summer months. The company's position was that the plants were wild hemp, strictly rope-quality and barely worth the herbicide it would take to kill them. One August night, it all vanished, leaving not even stubble. The following morning, county mounties inquired. Other than admitting the unofficial Employee Arboretum had somehow disappeared, management disavowed all knowledge.

The rank and file pled memory loss: *Which particular acre of grass in Nebraska? And when the hell was yesterday?*

The summer went by in a string of freezing nights, and soon the first snowfall matched the perpetual winter indoors. On the Friday I decided to quit, huge flakes were falling. The grapevine carried this rumor, later confirmed by the in-house underground paper: the sheriff had notified our plant managers that a blizzard would close the roads and strand employees at the plant if they were not immediately released. Surely, we snarled, they would have to let our people go. We had not retained our faith in their humanitarian impulses, but this was a life-threatening situation.

Invisible factors, however, were at work. Not only did the lines keep moving, but the second-shift personnel were advised to come in, some from as far as eighty miles away, if they wished to continue enjoying the blessings of employment.

The reason for this entrapment was simple. The company had purchased, at fire sale prices, the stock of a defunct packing plant in Omaha. Higher-ups in management had been praying for a way to enforce overtime and process these poor extra cows into profits, when God sent them a blizzard.

At quitting time, only the antennas were visible in the parking lot, and the cars of second shift lined the ditches for eighty miles. In a rather moving since-you're-here-anyway, we're-all-in-this-boat-together speech, we were told that a golden opportunity to work all weekend was available for those inclined. (Which I was not particularly.) Meals would be free for the duration, and there were other special inducements. A line boss was dispatched to a nearby farm to purchase twenty pounds of Nebraska Numbweed for covert distribution. Rolling papers mysteriously appeared in the bathrooms like magic; cases of them. For two days, management went blind to crimes committed in the lockers or bathrooms. All this was reported as fact by the underground press, and confirmed by a score of my co-slaves. It happened. *J'accuse.*

A few hundred of us chose to abandon our cars and trek the five miles to the nearest plowed highway. On the way, we met a few snowpersons of the second shift, walking the other way. Knowing looks were exchanged, and we deserters trudged on into the whiteness, sustained by a vow that survivors would storm the general manager's office someday and garrote him with his own shiny intestines. The blizzard lasted until Sunday, but no one froze to death, and I quit the following week. So there's a happy ending.

Not as happy as it could be. I sense the Romans must have harbored a mild dislike for Carthage, to raze it, plow it under, and plant salt. I would prefer a giant asteroid flaming down from space tomorrow, obliterating the entire plant and the adjacent city across the river, sterilizing everything in a hellstorm, and leaving a bottomless lake to mark the spot. Sewage could then be dumped in, to ferment until the last tick of recorded time. Finally, a sign could be erected: *Puke City delenda est.*

# leaving the sea

## 0800

The Polish deep sea trawler *Parma* is drifting on a quiet sea, 48°27' north; 125°28' west, in Canadian offshore fishery zone five. The blue mountains between Carmanah and Bonilla Point are thirty sea miles off the bow.

*Parma* might be my last ship. I would be able to stop going to sea as a fishery observer on foreign ships and Canadian draggers if I could think what to do with my work clothes. This morning, I'm wearing a hooded green sweatshirt given to me by one of the deckhands on the Canadian black cod boat *Lana Janine*. The crew on the *Lana Janine* took to her life raft to save themselves last March outside Gowgaia Bay on the west coast of the Charlottes when the boat burned and sank after more than forty years fishing between Baja California and the Bering Sea. The green sweatshirt from the *Lana Janine* is stained with fish blood and smeared with grease from the stern winch now, but I cannot give it up yet.

The trawl winches are hauling our first codend, so I'm going on deck in a moment, wearing gumboots, of course, the pair an Alert Bay handline cod fisherman gave me one season when I was broke. The boots had appeared brand new on his deck, he told me, too small for anyone else. Must have been meant for me, he said.

Some Alert Bay fishermen gave me Fred Stanley's shirt, too, when I first started working at sea with the Poles and the Russians. They knew I was afraid of the foreign ships and figured Fred's sense of humor, as well as his infinite acquaintance with fish, might be transmitted to me through his red and black flannel shirt. Besides, they said, he collected flannel shirts, all identical. He'd never miss this one. Fred's shirt protected me through my first offshore voyages, then I gave it to Nikolai Sergeyevich, who needed its comfort even more than I did on the Soviet trawler *Mys Obrucheva*. Fred Stanley's shirt is probably still fishing on the Okhotsk Sea 2,000 miles from here. On *Parma*, my shirts are usually the same blue or green checkered cotton worn by every man on the ship except the officers on the bridge.

These past six years while I have been more at home on the sea than anywhere else, I felt the need to work in the same shabby Bering Sea coat liners and patched blue jackets the Russians wore, the same wool sweaters and yellow raingear the Poles used. Some days, though, when I stand for hours in the factory below decks measuring hake stomachs or testing the filleting machines, I wear pearls with these clothes.

## 1500

Afternoon dream: I am walking along Granville Street in Vancouver, wearing my work clothes, smelling of fish and blood, forbidden to get onto the Fraser Street bus. Panic thickens in my throat until I look down and see I am carrying *Parma*'s brass bell. This bell hangs from a steel frame on our bow and is so heavy that only a 25- or 30-degree roll could cause it to ring, but in the dream, it rests easily in my arms.

If there are no troubles on our ship in midafternoon, I lie down, still dressed, and float in a shallow sleep on my white-railed bunk in the hospital cabin on the passageway off the starboard side of the trawl deck. Deeper layers of sleep and the seagoing nightgown folded under my pillow are hours away. This white cotton, ankle-length nightgown, frilled at wrists and collar, has always satisfactorily contradicted the ship's hard edges for me and, I think, for the Russian and Polish fishermen who often saw it stuffed into my dirty jeans on deck in the dark when we trawled with our own heavy gear, hauling day and night. My nightgown is not beautiful or even white any more, but rust-marked from too many washings in distilled seawater running out of old pipes. Yet I am still glad to see it at night after the ship's steel and wood and wire all day.

## 2000

We have just finished supper. Tonight I ate in the crew's messroom, where aluminum knives and forks and spoons are jammed into a tin can set in the center of a long, oilcloth covered table. The trawl bo's'n, the deck crew, and I sit together on a bench, pretending we are a family, while Jesus standing on a green hill regards us with great gentleness from his picture pinned to the bulkhead above the coffee grinder. We had borscht and meat pies. I wore silver crescent-moon-shaped earrings.

## 2230

*Parma* is moving slowly across dark water to take our last haul of this day. In a minute or two, along with the fishermen, I will reach into the drying room for a black wool sweater unraveling at the neck. For a while yet, not much on the *Parma* will change. At dawn tomorrow, the ship will be close to her present position, and the day, like the one just gone, will be as fair and calm as any of us have ever known in these waters. *Parma*, who is old and whose crew fear for her in heavy seas, will steam serenely, her bell silent, firmly fastened to its rightful place on the bow. I will put on the Alert Bay boots and go down into the factory to see how the night's work has gone. Behind and below the huge fish tanks in the factory is the steering gear. Here, a wooden wheel is set alongside a 78° brass curve turning slowly on either side of a centered, broad, unmoving arrow in response to the helm and gyro-compass on the bridge, four decks above. The wheel, the arrow, and the curve of the steering gear are connected directly to the rudder, so we could, if need be, steer the ship from this deep place within her.

When I leave the sea and can no longer look at the steering gear and the bell on *Parma*, or any other ship, whenever I wish, I will need the green hooded sweatshirt from the *Lana Janine*, and the other hardworn work clothes, to help me remember.

# "Employees will be expected to have teeth and wear them daily to work."

— A rule issued by a Vermont ski resort after it fired a chambermaid who did not wear her dentures because they didn't fit properly. (February 1993 issue of *Labor Notes*)

TOBY SONNEMAN

# saving the family photographs

A full sixteen years after my first apple harvest, I found myself on a ladder again, picking a particularly abundant crop of golden apples. As I worked, I reflected on what had drawn me and my husband, Rick, to spend so many years of our lives as fruit pickers, and why it seemed so essential to give an account of our experiences.

Much had changed in those sixteen years since we began, but on that sunny day in October I was aware of how much had stayed the same. Physically I felt alternately exhilarated and exhausted by the hard work and the fresh air. Burdened with a heavy bag of apples that strained my back and shoulders as I walked to the bin, I often felt like a donkey carrying a load. But again on my ladder, looking out to the valley below filled with neat rows of fruit trees, and beyond to the snow-topped Cascade Mountains, I was awed by the beauty of this place. The apples themselves were lovely, a soft yellow color tinged with a rosy blush where the sunlight had left its mark. Although the physical work was hard and often monotonous, the surroundings made it a vastly more satisfying experience than factory work.

But it was later in the morning, when I'd stopped for a cup of coffee, that I was really reminded of why I'd been so drawn to this work. Rosie came by to chat with me. She had joined her husband, Bill, to work in supervising the harvest this year. Bill, originally from Oklahoma, had come to the Northwest as a child to pick fruit. Now he drove tractor and managed the orchard, but for decades he had made his living picking fruit, pruning, and thinning. He had a reputation as one of the fastest apple pickers around. Now his twenty-four-year-old son worked in the orchard and could pick as fast as Bill had.

Rosie started talking to me about an article Rick had written for the local newspaper, profiling several fruit pickers. One of them, she said, gave a bad image of pickers. In the article he'd complained about how little money he made and how hard it was to survive as a fruit picker. It made you feel depressed to read it, Rosie said, and that wasn't how she thought a picker ought to talk. "My family's always had a lot of pride in this work," Rosie asserted. "Billy's never been the sort to whine about anything, and if the day ever comes where he really feels bad about bein' in the orchard, well, that'll be the day he quits doin' this kind of work."

Rosie's argument moved me, bringing back all my years of living among fruit pickers and getting to know their ways. It reminded me why after reading John Steinbeck's *The Grapes of Wrath* in my youth I was so attracted to the migratory life and so glad to find that the people Steinbeck wrote about still existed. For all its hardships — low pay, low status, backbreaking work, and often poor conditions in the field and inadequate housing — most of the people who work in the fields and the orchards are not downtrodden, beaten individuals. "Fruit tramps" they call themselves mockingly, aware that mainstream society has derogatorily labeled them "tramps." Although they are regarded with disdain and encouraged by schools, communities, and government organizations to leave agricultural work rather than to improve it, these people have miraculously clung to their self-respect, believing in the dignity and value of their work. A sense of pride sustains them.

I am more realistic now than I was sixteen years ago when I had a somewhat romantic notion of migratory life, but the migrants' strong sense of pride still impresses me. It's what struck me when I first read *The Grapes of Wrath* in high school and wished I could know people like that — people who had such integrity and compassion for others that they could rise above the harsh way they were treated. Recently, rereading Steinbeck with the added perspective of years spent living and working with Okie migrants, I hear the ring of truth and accuracy in the voices and descriptions of the Joads. These were people who refused to be ashamed of the poverty and hardships that they endured; they would not think like victims, and they deplored any media reports that depicted them as "sorry, low-down fruit tramps."

The Okies were not my people, and though reading *The Grapes of Wrath* had awakened a longing to know the people Steinbeck wrote of, I thought that people like that had disappeared with the Great Depression. Becoming a fruit picker was not even a remote possibility for a Jewish high school student living on Chicago's South Side. It was not until I got to college that I could legitimize my interest in people with an academic term: anthropology. Like many of my generation, I was in college to learn for learning's sake, rather than to find a career. I knew I wanted to travel and I was very interested in migratory people. Independently, I read everything I could about Gypsies, and I got to know and photograph some Gypsies in the United States and Europe. But they had a distrust of a young *gaji* (Romani for a female "non-Gypsy") that kept me at a distance, and I realized that I couldn't get to know these people more deeply at that time in my life.

For several years I alternated adventure and travel with short stints at jobs to get by financially. In 1972 I was in limbo, without work or enough money to travel again. I was living in a dreary warehouselike structure in San Francisco with an assorted group of friends and strangers. Every day I'd go out to stand in long lines and fill out forms for the lowest-paid jobs. Despite my college education, my lack of experience in clerking, filing, or typing made the possibility of employment remote. It seemed time to leave the city, and when somebody mentioned that there were apricots to pick up north, I began to dream again of being a fruit picker.

Leaving my belongings at the San Francisco warehouse, I packed a small backpack and hitchhiked north. Rick joined me in Oregon, quitting his hated job at a pulp mill. He packed some clothes, a camera, and a blanket into his old VW bug, and together we continued north. In Seattle we made inquiries at the employment office. We were told there were picking jobs around Wenatchee, about 120 miles east of Seattle, so we traveled over the mountains, across Stevens Pass. It was one of the most beautiful trips I have ever taken. Waterfalls rushed down the Cascade Mountains, which separated the rainy western side of Washington from the drier hills and orchard country of central Washington.

In Peshastin, a tiny logging and orchard town nestled in the foothills of the Cascades, we found our first job. The lean old farmer in striped overalls who hired us led us to the cabin where we could stay while we worked. It was a simple two-room cabin. The kitchen was equipped with a woodstove and a hotplate, an old wooden table, and some battered pots and pans. The bedroom had a big, creaky double bed and a cot. In back of the cabin was a bathroom with a shower and toilet. That was a rare feature in a picker's cabin and seemed luxurious; later we were to live in several pickers' cabins with no facilities other than an outside water faucet and an outhouse.

Our first work was thinning. In early summer when the tiny apples and pears hang from the trees in clusters, it is time to thin them out, breaking up the clusters and spacing the fruit apart. The worker drops the smaller fruit to the ground so the remaining fruit can grow larger.

The work itself was simple, but learning to manage the ladders we used to reach the tops of the trees was often a challenge. The three-legged ladders were a nightmare to move on the steep foothill orchards.

We worked through the thinning season, then waited out the hot weeks of July and August while the fruit grew larger. We walked around the dry hills, swam in the icy river and the irrigation canals, and tasted tiny fresh strawberries from the farmer's garden and thick cream we bought from a neighbor. In mid-August we found another job and cabin and began the pear harvest, going to work at dawn, subjecting our backs to the strain of carrying the heavy bags of fruit.

By the time we were picking apples, the scorching summer days had cooled into crisp autumn ones. On frosty mornings we started to work at eight or nine, boosted by hot cups of coffee and cocoa. The work was never easy, but it began to have a rhythm and a pace that was becoming natural to us. The periods of total leisure in between the jobs, the breaks for coffee or lunch that had the qualities of a picnic in the orchard, and the seasonal changes in the work and the weather made us feel integrated with the land and the seasons and seduced us into the fruit-picker way of life. Soon we were thinking of the next season, the next job, the next fruit to pick.

We began to meet people who were unlike the more settled people in a community. The migrants were free of the stresses and constraints of highly structured time, the appropriate dress required for higher-status jobs, or the acquisition and upkeep of all the trappings of middle-class life. Most of the pickers we met were Okies — a mixture of people whose parents had left Oklahoma, Arkansas, Texas, and Missouri to follow the crops in the 1930s. They had a distinct way of speaking that was often humorous and unexpectedly eloquent and a connection with their extended families that was unusual in the West. Their hardiness and sense of humor seemed to pull them through the worst circumstances intact and always made a good story later. We found the Okies to be great storytellers, and the tales they told of their varied experiences lured us into trying the fruit run.

After that first season in Washington, we traveled south to Florida to pick oranges and grapefruit. Here we experienced some of the worst elements of the migrant's world. The work was incredibly hard. It took me most of that first season in Florida to learn to move the heavy wooden twenty-foot ladders just a few inches at a time so they wouldn't topple over. As I am just over five feet tall, the ladders towered over me. The weighty citrus fruit grew on tall trees with thorns so treacherous that pickers had to wear thick leather gloves to protect their hands. Picked fruit was carried in huge bags with one strap across the neck and shoulder, a bag design that eventually crippled the older workers. The sandy orchards, called *groves* in the South, were a nightmare of biting insects, ants, and spiders. Cars got stuck in the loose sand, and it was a challenge to walk in the sand carrying ladders and heavy bags of fruit.

On top of this, the crews were incredibly inefficient: sometimes we spent days waiting for a bin in which to dump our fruit, while the crew boss and the tractor driver played endless games of cards. The crew bosses in Florida were often dishonest and exploitative, especially on the "wino" crew we worked with our first year there.

Perhaps worst of all was the prejudice and hostility of the surrounding community. We were denied motel rooms, use of public restrooms, and apartment rental when it was known that we picked fruit, and we soon learned to hide our occupation. The rampant discrimination gave us a small taste of what life is like for the black people in the South, for whom fruit picking is one of the only forms of employment. Crews were basically segregated, with the exception of one fully integrated crew that held a union contract: the United Farm Workers crew for Coca-Cola (Minute Maid). Although as whites we were able to find work with crews that were otherwise all black, we saw few other whites interested in doing this, and we suspected that a black person would not have the same freedom to work on a white crew.

But even in Florida, where conditions were the worst, both black and white fruit pickers reflected a pride in their work. As Rick worked alongside other pickers, he often asked if he could take their pictures. These early photos were often self-consciously posed as the pickers tried to look their best for the portraits. Yet the poses they struck accurately revealed their self-perceptions. With straightened backs, their shoulders arched back and their heads held high, the pickers would look piercingly into the lens of the camera. They were often on or next to their ladder. Never once was there any expression of shame or disgrace in the work that they were doing. And as recently as last fall, when I went around the orchard taking pictures of the apple pickers, many of whom were Hispanic, the pose was the same, as if their sense of pride crossed all cultural lines.

Our first winter in Florida, after much persistence, we were lucky enough to get a job on the UFW crew (we tried to get on the next winter as well, but as migrants we had lost our seniority). There we met Walter Jay Williams, a thirty-five-year-old steward for the union. Walter was an Okie from a small community in Texas. When he was a boy his father had built a camper from flattened tin cans, and with the camper nailed to a wooden frame on the back of a Model T Ford pickup truck, he had taken the family to California to pick cotton, peas, and fruit. Walter's mother had a collection of old photographs from that time, and years later Walter borrowed the photos from his mother so that Rick could make copies of them for the rest of the family. These photographs were a treasured record of the family's journey west and the roots of their new lives as migrant fruit pickers in the 1940s and 1950s.

Walter liked to tell a story about the time when he was a boy and the trailer they were then living in veered off the road as they drove around a difficult curve on a mountain pass. Their possessions were scattered about the road and the family surveyed the wreckage with dismay. But Walter's mother, wasting no time, ran down the road to rescue the family photographs that had tumbled out of their box before the relentless wind blew them away forever. The image of this story stayed with us, a symbolic message of the importance of remembering the history and experiences of these people.

Walter himself was an endless source of stories and experiences, a wealth of oral history. He had been a preacher in Texas and he had a strong sense of righteousness and religious values. He was unusually well read and open-minded and his vision of fruit picking as dignified work made him an eloquent speaker for other migrants. In Florida he seemed in his element as a union organizer, using the style and the language of preaching to motivate both the blacks and the whites on the crew who protested union dues even though their wages were double those of nonunion crews.

After meeting Walter, we often went to visit him and his family, and they welcomed us with a generous hospitality. Walter, Matte, and their six tow-baited children lived in a mobile home on the outskirts of a little town. Walter told us that he wasn't able to make the payments on the mobile home — he'd probably let it just "go back." Anyway, he wanted to travel again. He spoke longingly of cherry picking and told us of the places in California, Oregon, and Washington where they'd picked. "Once those cherries start bloomin', you couldn't hardly keep me here," Walter said.

We left Florida in the early spring with no more money than we'd come with. We felt lucky to have enough to leave on. We weren't too serious about fruit picking yet, so we took odd jobs in California and visited friends there.

June came, and we weren't committed to other jobs or settled in a particular place. We remembered what Walter had said about cherry picking and we wondered if we could really make money picking them. We traveled to Kennewick, in southern Washington, and began looking for jobs. We remembered Walter talking about a good cherry-picking job he had for a Japanese orchardist in Kennewick, but we had no idea how to find him. The orchards were widely scattered around a large area, and we hardly knew how to look for a job. We were outside town, filling our car with gas and wondering where to go next, when a pickup truck and a camper pulled up near us. The children's heads poking out the window reminded us uncannily of Walter's kids. Taking a long shot, we asked the driver of the truck if he knew of them. Yes, he answered, he was Walter's cousin, and he gave us directions to the orchard where Walter was working. Although this seemed to us a fortuitous chance meeting, we later realized that Walter and his cousin James (whom we later came to know as well) saw nothing remarkable in the event. There were so many interrelations between families on the migrant run that they assumed you could eventually find anyone you were looking for. For us, however, since we had no knowledge or experience in the orchards and no connections to other fruit pickers, the coincidence seemed providential.

Walter was delighted to see us, and he managed to get us a job at the orchard he was working in. We parked our VW van alongside the trailers and buses and tents and set up our camp. In the morning Billy, the foreman, showed us where to pick and found ladders and buckets for us. After struggling for half a day only filling a few boxes, while we watched pickers around us fill stacks of boxes with cherries, we found Walter and his family and asked for help. We spent some time just watching them while they gave us tips on cherry picking. By the next day, our boxes were stacking up faster, although it looked as if we'd never catch up to the pickers who'd been at it for years.

After working in Kennewick, we found out about other cherry jobs in the Northwest and tried to work with the Williams family whenever we could. Our affinity with this extended family developed as we continued to spend time around them. Sharing coffee breaks and lunch breaks in the orchard, spending afternoons after work, playing and reading with the children, and listening to Walter's stories in the evening, we grew very close to them.

As we were becoming drawn into the cycles of the fruit run, the Williamses were unofficially adopting us into their family. We met Walter's younger brother, Daniel; his wife, Darlene; and their six children. Daniel's family also picked fruit and often parked their trailer right next to Walter's in the migrant camp. Despite the differences in their styles, the two families lived close to each other, without much privacy, in relative harmony. Later we met another of Walter's brothers, Paul. He lived in Texas and had to be on a kidney-dialysis machine, but he loved to pick fruit and missed it so much that one year he came out to pick for a week with his wife, Bonnie, and their two children. He thought cherry picking was worth the long trip from Texas to Washington, even though he had to spend two of the days in Washington traveling more than a hundred miles from the cherry orchard to be hooked up to the nearest dialysis machine. Paul's obvious attachment to fruit picking was a stunning example of the pickers' attitudes toward their work. It differed greatly from what we'd been led to expect. These were not people forced into agricultural work by unfortunate circumstances. These were people making a choice, valuing the opportunity to stay connected with their families. They were choosing a way of life considered to be without merit by the rest of society.

In the years that followed, we became initiated into the migrant culture through Walter, his family, and friends. We saved our picking money to buy our own first trailer — a little sixteen-footer from the 1950s — which we pulled with a 1956 pink and white Buick. The wooden interior of the trailer made us feel like we were living in the hollow of a tree. With a little dining booth, a compact kitchen, and a bed — all within arm's reach — the trailer was cozy and functional, and we discovered how much we liked the freedom of our own migratory home.

We wintered in Florida, Texas, Arizona, and Washington. Every year we hitched up our trailer in late April or early May and traveled to California for the first of the cherries, then followed the fruit as it ripened up north and east to Montana. We picked prunes, pears, and apples in central Washington and stayed until the cold and the lack of work drove us south again.

Most of our jobs were only a couple of weeks long, but we came back to the places that had been good to us year after year. We worked with many people that we knew and met new ones at each job. We were amazed at the interconnected relations of the people who worked the fruit. It seemed like a large extended family. We were continually reminded how many people picked fruit because they loved it — not because they had to.

Times were changing for the fruit pickers though. Jobs were getting scarce, real wages lowering. The growers in northern California and the Northwest had increased their use of illegal aliens, most of them workers from Mexico, and they became the preferred choice for cheap, reliable labor.

In 1975, we helped form Migrant Workers of America, an advocate group for migrants. We hoped that fair legislation could preserve the jobs and lifestyle so crucial to this culture. We continued the organization for several years, learning some difficult lessons in the process. Few legislators cared about migrants; because they were migratory they were not represented by any particular political candidate, and often they did not vote at all. Migrants had difficulty planning where they would be at election time in order to establish state residency in advance. This, coupled with their alienation from local issues and politics, proved to be a real obstacle in our discussions with legislators. In any case, fair legislation began to seem impossible; as workers of different races were pitted against each other, the real issues were obscured. And finally, Okie migrants were among the least organizable of groups — they were too suspicious of organization and too protective of their individual independence to participate in group action. These conflicting factors began to undermine the intent of the organization, and in 1978 the group disbanded.

We continued to pick fruit, however, and in the spring of 1979 our first child was born. We took him with us to the cherry orchard in Kennewick when he was just six weeks old. Our new definition as a fruit-picking family deepened our acceptance and involvement with other fruit pickers. At last our co-workers realized that we weren't picking fruit as a lark or a fill-in job, or as a means to writing a book. Despite our cultural, educational, and hereditary differences we had become, like them, wed to the seasons and the life of the fruit run.

In recent years we have watched and have been affected by the dying

of that lifestyle. Orchards have been gobbled up by subdivisions and con-
dominiums with names like "Cherry Tree Acres." Small growers with personal relationships to the workers are forced to sell out, and agribusiness con-
glomerates take over. Workers are no longer valued for their reliability in
coming back year after year or for picking the fruit with care. With lowered
wages, and large numbers of recent immigrants who desperately need work,
many Okie migrants have been pushed out of fruit work. Often they are
unable to find jobs in orchards where they have previously worked. Contractors supply a large grower with a ready crew, and often such contractors
favor non-English-speaking workers because they are frequently in a position where they must accept less than adequate conditions and wages.

The situation in farm work changes year by year as new immigration
laws are enacted, affecting the use of illegal workers, but many of the
people we worked with in the fruit orchards have left, finally discouraged
by lack of work and the drop in wages. Many of them have returned to
Texas, Oklahoma, Arkansas, and Missouri, where land is still cheap and
they are among their own people. Daniel Williams returned to Texas with
his wife, Darlene, to pursue his occupation as a roofer. Walter Williams
also left the fruit run many years ago. After his marriage to Mattie broke
apart, he became a traveling preacher once again in Texas and later hap-
pily remarried. Now, as an ordained minister with a church in Artesia, New
Mexico, he feels he has found his true calling. A recent letter from him
demonstrates that he still retains a strong feeling for his fruit-picker past.
"Even if the years have separated me from the fruit fields of my childhood,
they can never take them out of my blood," he wrote, "because it flows in
my veins like life itself."

Other fruit pickers have settled in the West, in towns in California,
Oregon, Washington, and Idaho, finding other kinds of work to sustain
them and perhaps still picking fruit in the summer. Even those who leave
are often drawn back temporarily, their fingers itching to pick fruit again,
their spirits eager for the expansive freedom of the road. We are now
among this group of fruit pickers. Rick is a journalist for a small-town newspaper in Washington, and I am an independent writer and artisan. But every summer I drive to the surrounding cherry orchards at the break of dawn
— 4:30 A.M. — and slip into my old harness and bucket for the yearly
ritual of cherry picking. There are always familiar faces in the orchard,
people we have known for fifteen years or more. We've watched their children grow, and they have known our children since they were babies lying under the fruit trees.

Perhaps they are ordinary people, but in the context of our changing society they seem extraordinary — remarkable for their wit, perceptiveness, and ability to survive. We've often been reminded of Walter's mother, running down the road to save the family photographs before they blew away. Much of this way of life has been eroded, leaving only the memories. As Walter writes, "Just knowing that there was such a life and I was a part of it is reason enough to feel a sense of pride."

A COSMOPOLITAN survey of 106,000 women found that single women make more money than married women, have better health, and are more likely to have regular sex.

— From *Backlash: The Undeclared War Against American Women* by Susan Faludi, copyright 1991, Crown Publishers, Inc.

WILLIAM JOHNSON

# snapbeans

There was a green
glistening mound
beyond the washtub.
Autumn — I'd crawl
beneath her apron,
legs pale under
muslin, veins like
runners of beanvines
musty with talcum,
wiry, clutching for
light. Above me
a sound like
a slingshot, each
pod delivered of
its sweet split
second of song.
Later, the kitchen
was a steaming
cannery. She tamped
each jar with paraffin,
clamped it, then
twisted the bright
gold ring. All night
sugar-bloom and pectin
pressed out oxygen,
the *plink* when
a lid cooled sealing
her love in the dark.

*Frank Wood's family, Toksook Bay village, hunting birds and eggs in 1981, before hunting at the time of egg laying was prohibited.*

*Always Getting Ready: Upterrlainarluta,* © 1993 by James H. Barker. Excerpted by arrangement with University of Washington Press.

# subsistence

For many Yup'iks, subsistence activities teach children much more than hunting and fishing; they convey respect and proper conduct toward the land and water and animals and other humans; they promote satisfaction from hard work and contribution to the kin group. For many Yup'iks, subsistence goes beyond mere economy — it is a vital way of life and a source of pride and identity.

...

...the fish-cutting table stands by a slough that passes the other side of the camp. Sylvia and Anesia were there working in the usual costume, rain pants and aprons made from plastic garbage sacks. They were cutting king salmon into strips or wide double-fillets called "blankets."...Each woman has learned from her mother or grandmother precisely how to cut fish for the weather conditions and drying methods of her area.

...

In the hunting and processing of wild fish and game, Yup'iks actuate their relationship with the natural world. Some expressions of these relationships seem esoteric today, fractured and out of context, especially to youth. Still, there are Yup'ik men who silently and gratefully provide a drink of fresh water to a seal, believing that the seal offered itself to the hunter because he would assure proper and respectful dispatch and processing, beginning with the quenching of its thirst.

...

We traveled the nine miles to the frozen shore and then ten more miles out on the ice....There was little open water and the ice pack was unsafe for further traveling. Joe did find one pond of open water about a hundred yards across. Kneeling behind a chunk of ice he scratched the butt of his rifle against the ice, a sound that entices the curious seal. One popped up. He shot the seal and quickly retrieved it.

...

In the mid-1800s Yup'iks were organized into approximately twenty kin-based societal groups or *tungelquqellriit*, meaning "those who share ancestors (are related)." The most socially significant and economically effective units of

*Melvin Tony, James Tony, and John Chikigak, all from Alakanuk, traveling on the Yukon.*

membership were related, extended (three generations) families or *ilakellriit.* …Yup'iks were the last of Alaska's Native groups to have sustained contact with non-Natives.…Technological and material introductions, easily discussed and generally appreciated are the most tangible evidence of change.

. . .

…Sebastian zigzagged to stay with the whale and at one point the others yelled to him to keep out of the line of fire. Harpoons were thrown and a rope snarled in someone's prop. Boats careened around each other as they followed the desperate attempts of the beluga to escape.

. . .

The fishcamp survives from earlier, more nomadic times when Yup'ik families moved several times each year in pursuit of foods.…The camp can be as simple as a single whitewall tent, a smokehouse, and a fish rack with the cutting table nearby. More established camps will have substantial cabins, outbuildings, smoke houses, rows of drying racks, steam baths, and gas-powered Maytag washers.

. . .

Our Bethel judge, Chris Cooke, once heard the case of an elderly man accused of killing a beaver out of season.…"I asked him if he had anything to say on his own behalf before sentence was imposed since there is a defense of necessity (need for food). At that point he said he'd been out

*Arlene and Cynthia Tunutmoak pick edible greens, Black River fishcamp.*

camping and hunting on the Tuluksak River for a number of days and that he'd broken his false teeth and couldn't eat, couldn't chew his food. He wanted to use the beaver's teeth to replace his false ones and that the beaver teeth were very good for that."

*Boys with birds, Nightmute.*

. . .

The basic western scientific tenet that wildlife can be managed draws incredulity from some Yup'iks; humans should not be so presumptuous and arrogant lest animals and fish make themselves scarce.

*Mike Uttereyuk butchering beluga, Black River fishcamp.*

. . .

"Someone turned me in for killing a moose out of season. The State knew that it is impossible to get store goods into Lime Village in winter, but they took the moose meat away and fined me $50. I think it is odd

*Sophie Amadeus covering fish, Umkumiut fishcamp.*

that I hunt by foot with moccasins on and am tried for hunting for my family when they are hungry, and airplanes land all the time right in front of my village, shoot moose and caribou, cut off the heads, and take off, leaving the meat behind."

STEPHEN J. BEARD

# "imagine a stack of blocks..."

## AN INTERVIEW WITH
## DAVID JAMES DUNCAN

David James Duncan's The River Why, *published in* 1983 *by the Sierra Club and later by Bantam Books, is a passionate examination of fish and fishing within the context of rapidly growing cities and quickly deteriorating fish habitat. It has been compared to such unexpected modern classics as J. D. Salinger's* The Catcher in the Rye, *Joseph Heller's* Catch 22, *and Robert Pirsig's* Zen and the Art of Motorcycle Maintenance. *Duncan's second novel,* The Brothers K, *published by Doubleday in* 1992, *again displays his originality and passion, this time through an epic of family strife, love of baseball, and the social chaos occasioned by the war in Vietnam.*

*Duncan himself was the classic starving artist for almost twenty years, working odd jobs and running a lawn-care business known as The Lawn Ranger while inventing his career as a novelist. In this interview, he discusses success, its meaning, and the passion and practice of his literary life.*

**Steve Beard:** When we had the conversation setting up this interview, you said something you'd like to talk about was the paradox of success. What did you mean by that?

**David Duncan:** Well, there's a line in *The Brothers K* quoting Tony Gwynn, the great hitter for the San Diego Padres, who said, "Once you're where you think you want to be, you're not there anymore." That's the paradox. Writing a novel that's as good as you can make it, and having it published and well-received, that's a dreamlike scenario for a lot of people. But the realization of that dream puts you in kind of a tenuous position, because once the dream is realized, it's no longer the carrot you were plod-

45

ding along toward. So you rather quickly need to substitute another carrot, build a new dream.

SB: So when you're done, there's a kind of "now what?" reaction?

DD: A little bit of that. I think the paradox that surrounds so-called success is that if a new goal isn't set pretty quickly, if you don't shoulder a new burden, you enter a flaccid state. There's something insipid, spiritually, about success. For several months after *The Brothers K* was published, I had to go from bookstore to bookstore appearing to revel in having finished this massive novel. That was fun a few times, but fairly quickly I was in danger of repeating myself. Rather than expressing spontaneous feelings, I was performing a little skit about how I felt about finishing, when in fact I'd finished the book some months before. I think movie actors probably go through the same thing. They're trying to express enthusiasm and spontaneity and freshness about a project they finished a year ago. That's just the way the film process works. It wasn't quite as bad for me because *The Brothers K* was brought out in a hurry. I finished writing it in September of '91 and it was a book in the spring of '92. But it was still an awkwardness.

SB: I understand that you used to be pretty obsessive about your work. That if you had a week to write, you'd sometimes work all night and all day for a couple of days and then just collapse.

DD: My work pattern has been to work very long days, day in and day out, primarily because creative flow is such a tenuous thing. For me, anyway. Sometimes I get up in the morning and for no explicable reason even passages from books that I love are just dead. There's no music to them, it's like someone threw a cloth over the strings on a guitar, there's no resonance. When that happens, I can't work. But when the resonance is there, when I feel the narrative drive singing, I push myself as hard as I can, to take advantage of the fact that music is playing.

SB: Do you do that now? I mean, you're married, you've got young children...

DD: On *The Brothers K*, I got a little more sedate. The rhythm of the work came to revolve around my biweekly visits with my son, who lives at the coast. I knew that I'd be driving down to get him and for those three or four days I would take off and spend time with the family. And then for another nine or ten days, I worked twelve hours a day again.

SB: There was a quote about obsession in *The Brothers K*. It goes, "Technical obsession is like an unlit, ever-narrowing mine shaft leading straight down through the human mind. The deeper down one plunges, the more fabulous, and often the more remunerative, the gems or ore. But the deeper down one plunges, the more confined and conditioned one's thoughts and movements become, and the greater the danger of losing one's way back to the surface of the planet." Now, that was about Roger Maris hitting sixty-one home runs in 1961 and how it affected him as a baseball player — at least that's what it was about directly — but it was obviously indirectly about some other things. Like writing a novel?

DD: The experience of writing a novel…well, here's a visual image. Imagine picking up little wooden blocks, scores of them, tiny ones, until you've got a stack of them three or four feet high. You've got like hundreds of them stacked up, and you're holding them in your hands, balancing them. A novel is just that intricate. When you're working hard, you've created a stack of images in your mind that's as structurally complex as this physical image I'm trying to make. And when you're interrupted, you have to take the whole stack of four of five hundred things and set it down. Chances are it will come tumbling down on itself when you do that, so you have to pick it up again, trying to remember how you stacked it the first time, knowing it might not be the same. This is why fiction writers often have such desperate looks on their faces when friends come knocking on their doors.

Obsessiveness is dangerous. But I feel that a certain kind of relentlessness is crucial to the novel-writing process. I mean, you need to find out what the limits are as far as what your family will tolerate, what your body will tolerate, and whether you're really working as close as you can to those extremes. But if you're being mild about the whole thing, I'd have to question how much progress you're going to be able to make. There *are* a few writers who sound like it comes easier to them. Tom Robbins talks about how he works from ten in the morning to three in the afternoon and then plays for the rest of the day, but I would guess that from ten to three, you know, he must be a real maniac.

SB: To change the subject a little bit, I think it is pretty obvious that there are negative aspects to success as a writer. But what do you see as the most positive things that have happened to you as a result of *The River Why* and *The Brothers K*?

DD: Well, I'm now able to make a living doing a kind of work that feels so central to me that I'd do it as often as possible whether I was able to make a living at it or not. I led the starving-artist life for almost twenty years. I now have a contract that's moved me up to, I don't know, high school teacher wages? Which sure as hell beats the McDonald's wages I was making. So that's a big, flagrant blessing, being fairly paid to do work from the heart, work I can pour my whole being into. That's a positive that's hard to beat.

SB: Are there others?

DD: A lot of the jobs I used to have felt bad to me. I mean, I worked in a plastics factory for a while once. And I was a janitor at a place that had a lot of defense contracts. Being somewhere to the left of Dave Foreman [founder of Earth First!], it's a relief for me to not be doing that kind of thing, some form of work that's environmentally damaging. I drove a cardboard recycling truck around the time I sold *The River Why*, so even though some trees are coming down to create these books, I feel karmic balance in the fact that I recycled many, many tons of corrugated.

SB: So you paid for it like that, made up for it?

DD: Well, I'm being whimsical, you know. But...well, do you know about the Jains? They're a religious sect in India who take no forms of life, who only eat food that is somehow cyclic. They wouldn't eat carrots, for example, because they'd have to pull the whole carrot and kill it, but they would eat corn, because they could just pick the ear and the plant is still alive. They wear gauze masks over their faces so they don't inhale insects and kill them. All kinds of things. Actually, I think a good course in microbiology would do the Jains a lot of good. To see all those white corpuscles wasting innocent germs, antibodies kicking the shit out of foreign bodies! There's a bloody Godzilla movie going on inside of us all the time, and no gauze mask can change that. But the Jains are the only people I know of who are *really* serious about making the most pacifistic environmental impact possible. And I'm not quite a Jain. I believe we all, Jains included, live by sacrifice. I believe there's a way of picking and eating carrots that allows the carrot to forgive you. And I believe there's a way of writing that allows the sacrificed tree you're writing on to forgive you, too. There is such a thing as wanton writing, writing that is not worthy of a tree's death. But what literature, at its best, enables human beings to do is a huge boon to all life forms, I think, I hope, I pray. The reader, to my mind, is like the conductor of a symphony. The orchestra is the imagination, the book is the score; and when a person sits down with a book and starts conducting, it's really an incredible skill, if you stop to think about it. A person sits down with a book, and there's no sound, no instructions, no real clues as there are on sheet music as to how the lines should be expressed. There are only these dead words on a page. And the reader lifts this deadness and runs it through the imagination in a way that brings a world, and all these emotions, and all this complexity, to life. To me, it verges on the miraculous that so many people have the power to do this. Fiction is virtually an ontological proof of the Inner Life. And the greater a person's respect for the Inner Life, the greater their respect for *all* life.

SB: So what are you doing now? Are you doing something similar to what you had going with *The Brothers K*, two or three things at once?

DD: Wo-he-lo. That's Girl-Scoutese for "Work Health Love," and that's what I'm doing. I've got a contract with Doubleday that says I'll write two more novels in the next four and a half years, roughly. Obviously not on the scale of this monster [lifts *The Brothers K*]. I've also got a newborn baby daughter who has colic. Wo-he-lo! That means, "Woe, Hell, Lookout!"

SB: Can you tell me what you're going to write about?

DD: I think it is painfully obvious that we're living in a time of massive transformation. There's a period in Northwest Indian mythology called the transformation era. That's the time when Raven went from being white and having a beautiful voice to being seared by fire, turning black and getting his present *Grawwnk*. I want to look at the present in a way that combines elements of fiction and elements of mythology. I want to write a work of fiction that deals with issues like intentional communities and bioregionalism without using buzzwords like "intentional community" and "bioregionalism." I hate the buzzwords, but I love the fact that the people who bandy these words about are struggling to find the way that my son and daughters are going to be able to live; and I'm interested in finding that way of life myself. Right now, my new book is a stew about a bunch of people in the present days urbs and burbs whose lives aren't working, who have huge frustrations for some reason or other. But rather than just take them through the paces of a black end-of-civilization-as-we-know-it comedy like Vonnegut's *Hocus Pocus*, I want to honestly try to focus on what might come next. To fill the gulf between the West of today and the West Ursula Le Guin foresees in *Always Coming Home*, for example. I mean, life with the Kesh would be, will be, great. But I'm fascinated by some of the mundane transformation questions. Nuts and bolts stuff. Like how we got rid of the IRS. And the Columbia River dams. And what killed enough of us off to keep the region inhabitable. Day-after-tomorrow prophecy.

SB: What do you think this transformation we seem to be going through will mean in terms of having a job, for example?

DD: The idea of *job*, of people being paid, being employed, has all kinds of political clout. But employment itself is not The Good. Genghis Khan's horsemen, for example, all had jobs. And a lot of raped women and dead children would have preferred them to be unemployed. Oregon and Washington loggers crying about loss of work once the trees are gone, however, strike me as analogous to ninetenth century soldiers from Fort Apache crying about unemployment after the Indians were all dead. We need to see an end to destructive jobs. Let certain types of work die their dinosaur deaths. I've had twenty kinds of jobs myself, and I've been laid off, fired, and have joyously quit many of them. My experience is that it's easiest to find new work if you don't resist change.

SB: Then you see certain kinds of jobs disappearing as something that will continue.

DD: Part of what I see coming is incredibly dark. I hope I'm wrong, but that's how I feel. I look at things like the Wise Use Movement, and I feel a lot of us are not getting smart enough fast enough. These people are so addicted to habit and so resistant to change. The Wise Ass Movement — as I like to call it — is just a politically organized failure of the imagination. And when the imagination fails on a scale that wide, the laws of nature and of karma have no choice but to make humans and animals and the earth itself suffer the consequences on the same massive scale. North America never was and never will be just an agglomeration of resources for "us" (industrial collaborators) to "use." North America is just a bad name for an astoundingly beautiful mosaic of mountains, rivers, deserts, and valleys, the health of each of which affects the health of the whole. The sooner we all realize this, the better. And in order for us to realize this, a lot of the old pioneer myths and laws and politics are going to have to die.

SB: How does that play into the novel you're writing?

DD: It doesn't, directly. I'm not going to write about the dark side of the present transformation, because I believe the ultimate outcome of this transformation is going to be extremely positive. This is, in part, why my next book is a comedy. The book will also raise odd questions, and not necessarily answer them, or perhaps only answer them in traditional, nonliterary ways. Why did Raven agree to save Noah by ending the Flood? Why did Coyote decide to bring down the American insurance industry? How did he do it? But I'm starting to steal my book's thunder.

Native Americans traditionally taught that the greatest measure of a culture's morality is the impact its actions have on persons living seven generations later. By that standard, most modern Americans have never experienced a genuine culture. I hope to confuse the industriousness clean out of a few such Americans with a moral, native comedy.

JOHN STRAWN

# the whirling man

antiago's fearful atmosphere rivals Mexico City's purulent, coruscating air. In late January, the middle of the Chilean summer, smoke from thousands of acres of forest fires burning wild in the coastal mountains blends with Santiago's hydrocarbon effluent in a mean, corrosive fusion. There are 14,000 buses in this city, and with each nudge forward in halting traffic a bus spits out a puff of blue-gray smoke.

Santiago sits on the plain of a great valley that runs between the high interior mountains of the Andean cordillera and the lower range stretched along the coast. Without wind, as on this day, the air is tangible, a scratch, bronchial sandpaper. On the kind of day Charles Darwin had described 160 years ago as "truly Chilean: glaringly bright" — an excess of UV rays, of course, adding to the ambiance here in the ozone-depleted south — we ordered a typically Chilean lunch, heavy on bread and meat, with Fanta to douse the grit, and settled in to chew and swallow under the umbrellas of a restaurant terrace.

Above the aural bruises of the traffic, I caught the high-pitched tones of a loud whistle. Across the street, a man with a tripod-mounted grinding wheel slung over his shoulder, like a hod, was serenading in front of an apartment building. The scissors sharpener, making his rounds.

Then I heard a drumbeat, a clumsy cadence, a stumbling but insistent rhythm. The sounds drew my eyes and ears east, in the direction of the drainage ditch called the San Carlos Canal — hidden, here in the colonels' neighborhood of Los Leones, behind white stuccoed walls. Water gray as slate coursed through the canal toward the Rio Mapocho, the open sewer flowing through Santiago. Away through the haze, on the crown of San Cristobal, the statue of the Virgin Mary — the only virgin in Santiago, the natives joke — gathered in supplicants, beset by wrought-iron racks of flickering votive candles.

Coming toward us, I saw a man and a boy, father and son, each bearing a drum on his back, each holding a pair of drumsticks under his arms. The skins on the drums were transparent, and through each ran a thin rope, connecting the ankle of the drum-bearer to a cymbal mounted atop the drum. A one-man band and his shadow, the one-boy band. The father flapped his arms, a mock chicken, and with each wave of his hands the drumsticks beat a thick tattoo behind him. The shadow, a tiny boy of five or six, battered out a slow tune, biting his lower lip in concentration, neither smiling nor afraid.

His father, keeping the beat with his left arm, reached out to rotate the boy with his right, turning him in a tight arc. The boy planted a foot, like a basketball player, and started to pivot, his tiny cymbals collapsing with each rotating step. The father nodded, expressionless, as the boy turned. The sound had no music, a barrel of metal filings rolling down a hill. After a dozen turns, the boy stopped and looked toward his father. The man had on a crushed felt hat, a red T-shirt, and torn blue pants. The boy wore a baseball cap and had on a shirt that buttoned.

Their performance had, so far, caught only sidelong glances from the patio full of diners. The drivers of the cabs cued along the curb behind the drummer and his boy waited for the stylish ladies of Providencia Avenue to return from their shopping. None looked up from his *Mercurio*. Stretching his leg to check the fit of the rope running to his cymbal, the one-man band moved into an open spot of sidewalk twenty feet from where I sat. He flapped his arms with the pace of a quick heartbeat and started to turn, his ankle kicking out the cymbal's beat. The drum got louder and quicker as he started to spin. *Now* diners looked up from their plates. Faster and faster he spun, cymbals crashing, elbows accelerating, ready to lift or melt. Willing away vertigo, he turned, he whirled, he closed his eyes and spun. The boy never took his eyes off his father's twirling form.

And then he stopped, without a stagger, and walked toward the boy. His chest was heaving, his face covered with sweat. His black hair stuck straight out from the back of his hat, which he now pulled from his head. The boy squeezed his hat off the top of his head, too, crumpling it in his fists. Then he took it by the bill and tried to shape it into a bowl, but his hands were too small to make the motions well, and the back stayed rumpled.

The whirling man and his boy walked among the diners, holding out their hats. A man at the table next to mine took the boy's hand and gently rolled out the folds in his cap. Hold it this way, he said, and gently stroked the boy's head. Then he dropped in a pair of hundred-peso coins.

The boy turned and looked in my eyes. His skin was the color of creamed coffee, his eyes a liquid black. The whirling man's Andean profile was softened in his son. I felt at my pocket for coins, but it was empty. A thousand pesos is too much, I thought. I turned my face away from the boy. His father stood at my shoulder. I looked at his feet, the feet that danced across the pavement. They wore canvas shoes, filthy with the grime of Santiago, the soot of its lubricating air, the hydrocarbon syrup that coats your pores and glistens on your skin.

He was practiced in discerning intention. I had my own uncertainty to deal with. He nodded, the hint of a bow, and put his hand on the boy's back. They moved out of the terrace, and crossed the street behind the cabs. The man leaned down to speak to the boy, rattling a fistful of coins. I chewed, ashamed, but of what I couldn't be sure. I was not Chile, I was not Pinochet, I was not Pedro de Valdivia. I was a gringo, eating lunch, and I gave the whirling man nothing.

# words of work

### BODY RAIN

A tide of executives flooding the streets, desperately looking for a job, unemployed as the result of a corporate takeover.

### CRACK SPREAD

The margin between the price of refined products and crude oil.

### GOOSING THE BOWL

Buying massive quantities of a stock to raise its price.

High Steppers, Fallen Angels, & Lollipops by Kathleen Odean, copyright 1988, Dodd, Mead & Company, Inc.

### ACROBAT

In hosiery making, the part of a machine that moves up and down to finish a stocking.

### DUMB ROCK

A bomb without guidance systems, which just falls from a plane at high altitude.

### DUTCH LEAD

A lead sentence in a newspaper story which is total fantasy – a fact explained later in the story – but which dramatically sucks the reader into the story.

### DROOLING

Unrehearsed talking that fills unexpected gaps in TV and radio show transmissions.

Dictionary of Jargon by Jonathon Green, copyright 1987, Routledge & Kegan Paul.

SIBYL JAMES

# madame sévère, or teaching in tunis

Les *Étudiants:* My students, a total of nearly 300 in my classes. They lounge on the campus lawn between palm trees and stands of straggly flowers, between concrete buildings that were dingy the day they were built. They frequent the *buvette,* the snack bar where they elbow through crowds to the counter, waving chits to purchase endless sweets and caffeine. That same unruly chaos spills over into classes where they smoke and chatter, alternately polite and rude, interrupting discussions to shout out what they've learned already, brimming with theories gleaned from some previous teacher's lecture, some critic's work they've memorized. "Wasn't Ben Franklin a Deist?" one asks. "I don't know," I say, "I don't concern myself with the religion of leaders." Such heresy here, where the black leather jackets that practically constitute a uniform are sprinkled with the scarves the Islamic fundamentalist women wrap their heads in. The first week, by way of introducing ourselves, I ask, "What job do you want when you graduate?" and learn it's an idle question. They've been channeled all their lives, directed by exam scores into disciplines. Mine are the English language crew and will mostly end up high school English teachers, if they end up employed at all. Early into the term, they go on strike. Depending on whom I ask, they're either protesting poor living conditions in the school (food poisoning from the cafeteria, etc.) or the government's split-up of religion departments, thus reducing the fundamentalists' power. It's a pretty sweet strike; the students come to class to tell me they're not coming. Sometimes they're less considerate. One day I find the classroom empty. A student happens by and says they voted to start their holiday vacation early.

**A**cademic Equipment: Gritty blackboards, erased with an old wet rag I hate to touch, pick up gingerly each time, and so comb the Tunis stores until I find at last a true eraser. "Look," I tell my students proudly, displaying the eraser like an archaeologist's rare find. They're unimpressed; they're students; they don't have to erase the blackboards. But they do have to jockey for position in the room of photocopiers where boys (it is always boys) man machines that may print readably or not. I am obvious there, an older foreign face that spells professor. I could pull rank, eschew the niceties of queuing that nobody else respects. I wait my turn; I haul my papers from the briefcase that every student carries here, the briefcase that feels so alien to my American sixties self more accustomed to the shoulder straps of Guatemalan bags. I carry it self-consciously, like a child masquerading as a grown-up.

**O**f Zeros and a Plagiarism of Their Own: My students plagiarize; I give them zeros. "Madame, you are so severe." "Madame, we just copied the books' ideas, not the words." "Madame, we have no ideas, we have to copy." "Madame, since you've criticized President Hoover for refusing relief to the poor and unemployed, why don't you give us some relief on these grades?" "OK," I say, "I'll add some points because your Hoover analogy's so clever."

**P**aragraphs: My students don't believe in them. And don't believe in sentences either, sometimes write everything they have to say in one long continuous burst. No period or, as their British English names it, "full stop" between thoughts. Sometimes no thought. "Children," writes one, "are taught to watch t.v. before they are taught how even to put a book on one's lapses." "I think," claims another, "that all people would agree that the recognition of the justification of dictatorship is unanimously done. From this perspective, the recourse to dictatorship, by the government essentially, would be the best democratic reaction." In a dictatorship, a third continues, "the intellectuals are barred from revealing their ideas and their writings are often treated as revolutionary and that custody is the panacea to shut their big mouths."

**A**n Appropriate Diction: They don't like to discuss. They don't like to be asked for their own opinions. They want lectures, spoon-fed answers, and they want them heavily symbolic. "These sycamores in William Carlos Williams' poems," they say, "what do they stand for and why are there so many?" "They stand for trees," I answer, "and there must be a lot of them in Patterson, New Jersey." "That's stupid," reply the students. It's a coup to make them speak so directly and concretely. At first I thought their penchant for discourse in formal generalities was due to speaking in a non-mother tongue. Later I heard it linked to the attitudes that revere classical Arabic and mock the everyday Tunisian version, so students believe classroom language should be classic, formally profound. When they sit around my desk after school, discussing politics, they shed the classic, talk clearly human.

Exams: Come once, at the end of the year, and nothing else counts, not the essays I've spent hours grading, nor attendance — so there are always more students in the exam room than I've seen all year. Weeks before the exams, the teachers gather and slug the questions out. "Oh, yes," one says, "we want to have a question about heroism in *The Red Badge of Courage*, but we don't want to use the word 'heroism' in the question; that would make it too easy." We type the questions on official forms; after that, the teachers are out of the loop. Exams become a sort of lottery because the students don't take written tests in every course and administrative VIPs decide which questions will be used. I don't know the "winning numbers" till I stand before the class and open the envelope sealed with ritualistic red wax. The students know it's literature day, but that could mean British poetry, or Shakespeare, or the U.S. novel. So they gamble, prepare for some courses and not others. If they guess wrong and have nothing to say, they have to sit for an hour before they can write (in French, though this is the English department in an Arab country), "I'm turning in a blank page." I give one student my book of Robert Duncan's poems to read while he's sitting, waiting to turn in his blank page. The teachers stalk the room, performing what is called "invigilation," that is, keeping an eye peeled for cheating. My high heels strike an officious tapping on the concrete floor, a rhythm that makes students giggle; I begin to tiptoe. Invigilation means releasing students one by one to use the filthy bathrooms, and following them there. It means fighting the pretentiousness of some teachers so obsessed by rules and department rivalry that they question even the students' right to plastic cups of coffee, amenities considered somehow suspect, out of bounds. When the exam time's up, we nag the students, even comically pound their desks to make them hand their answers over. If they pass this written part, we'll face them across tables for the orals, in the humid heavy heat, all of us swatting flies.

Grading: Stacks and stacks of the same question from *The Red Badge of Courage*, a novel I don't like, and like less when I read that "this deconstruction of domestics foreshadows the absurdity of war that Henry himself is going to apprehend," or "Nature continues its diurnal intercourse, though sometimes obscure and dark," or "Henry fights unawares which proves that he is guided by thinking." I can see why many don't pass and many pass that never should. Anonymous exams with numbers below the ragged edge where the clerical staff have torn away the section where the students wrote their names (and their birth dates too because sometimes the names are so similar or the students write so illegibly or they spell their Arabic name so randomly in the French version that it doesn't match the administration's list, so the school needs another clue to identify them). After the grading, we'll spend hours matching up the numbers, paper-clipping each exam back to its name. I keep a list of marks, write nothing on the exams because another teacher will also have to grade them; then we'll meet over coffee and cigarettes or maybe couscous to compare and pick a mark between our differences or argue and read the exam again. There are twenty possible points; a student needs ten to pass and, by tradition, only Allah himself gets more than fifteen. Not much room to maneuver in. My first year, I think a failure's a failure and it doesn't really matter whether I write down seven or two. Later, I find it does. In the deliberations.

The Deliberations: They last forever, and some teachers come late so we can't start till midmorning (though we're told to arrive at 8:30 A.M.); some teachers leave early, and some don't show up. We sit with exams in front of us; one teacher reads the names, while others announce the grades for the various subjects. Some people say the numbers in French, and some in Arabic, so I'm caught off guard not knowing what they're talking about and don't realize it's my turn. The teacher who's maybe in charge adds the numbers up, and some get multiplied by coefficients of importance or perhaps difficulty or maybe whim. It's the total that matters, so a student who failed miserably in one course but aced another passes everything. Or maybe a student needed a failing seven to make a combined pass, but a teacher like me gave him only a two because a failure is a failure, how many degrees of it are there? Or perhaps a student's total falls inside the designated range for borderline. Ah, then it's possible to be "redeemed." And that's really the word that's used. We make a stack of "redeemables," then dig through the boxes of student records on green cardboard forms, checking the grades earned in class. At last, the rest of the year counts, if the student's done the homework, or if the male professors rushing over to look at a female student's photo think her face deserves redemption. We argue (but that's been going on all day) and we vote — with results that seem as

inexplicable as the ways of heaven. Sometimes a student who has been refused has better marks than one redeemed. When the arguments go on
too long in Franco-Arabe, I take breaks from the room of faculty judgment,
head for the campus lawn where students hang about all day, waiting ner-
vously for the names of those who passed to be announced on loudspeak-
ers, the voice like the muezzin's in the call to prayer. I pass some students
that I'm rooting for and flash them a surreptitious "OK" sign, a Western
gesture I later fear they've misinterpreted as zero. They know the rules of
passing are arcane, the system archaic. They know the reality of education here is chaos. They think it's all a governmental plot, a conspiracy to
keep them failing, repeating the same year over and over, because if they
graduate, there are no jobs.

# words of work

### DROP THE RUBBER JUNGLE
The lowering of rubber oxygen masks into an airplane cabin during an inflight emergency.

### CHERRY PIE
Extra work taken on by a circus worker to supplement his base income.

### COFFEE QUEEN
A third-rate gay prostitute who will sell his services for food and drink instead of money.

### COKULORIS
In filmmaking, a light diffuser spaced with irregular holes to give the appearance of "real" light.

### CYBERCRUD
The blinding of gullible or novice computer buyers with a torrent of jargon and esoteric fact.

### HOT BELLY
An abdominal problem that requires immediate, emergency surgery.

### MAP OF IRELAND
A hotel housekeeper's term for semen stains left on the sheets.

Dictionary of Jargon by Jonathon Green, copyright 1987, Routledge & Kegan Paul.

KENT CHADWICH

# sunday jazz

And you think of Jim who called
And how he said he stopped playing
That he'd sold the trumpet
At a fucking garage sale
Worden wails on tenor
And you blow angry
On a song you've practiced daily
And the gigs are good
Booked back-to-back today
The band is solid
Your CDs sell well, locally,
And there are forty in the tavern
Though a third are in the band
And the audience is friends
And your horn is hot this afternoon
And the players love the tune
And the music finds its legs
It leads you dancing through
Skittering the changes
And the young guys still have dreams
You nail that C for Jim
And on three hours sleep tomorrow
You'll balance office ledgers
And there's no living to be made here
But a life
And you're hep for each new set
And you know some songs you've carried
Will last longer than these walls
And you know you're just an eighth note
And goddammit eight make a whole

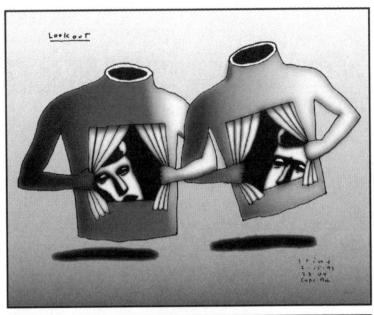

# turning point

When I look back over my first serious creative efforts, even as a kid, I worked without rhyme or reason. I made things because I loved to make things. That's all. I just threw myself and my efforts to the wind and hoped for the best. I had no method, no theme, no goal. The only thing that defined how or what I did were the limitations set by my tools and the degree of my enthusiasm.

For forty years I made art this way — sitting down, standing up, waving pencils, arms, brushes, paper-canvas-wood, printouts, videos — everything sailing around my studio, all of it trying to transport my creative impulses into the "real" world. It's been a slapdash affair at best. Somehow though, it worked. Out of this chaos, miraculously, has come enough good work that my basic needs as an artist and human being have been satisfied.

But something happened last month that put a new twist on things: I got run down and sick with the flu and had to spend some days in bed. While I was there I realized it was time to approach my creativity in a more methodical way. I thought this because my technology — pencils, oils, watercolors, airbrushes, ink, smoke (yes, smoke) and computers — had run me ragged. The computer, in particular, from my experience anyway, tends to encourage a kind of wild-horse, runaway-train working ambiance because of all the things it can do. I find it difficult to restrain from experimenting with that tool because it lends itself so easily to a "what if you try this" attitude. It doubled, maybe tripled, the trouble I was already encountering by giving my creative direction over to whim. It was clear something had to change.

Anyway, there I was in bed with my stuff spread all over the place: a clipboard filled with paper, my fountain pen, ink, pencils, a laptop, and a few books (among them *The Portable Jung*). All of it screaming out to be used. "I'm here. Try me. Use me. Read me."

But I did nothing, except think.

I think a lot. I'm not a good thinker though. By that I mean I'm not good at linear thinking, or thinking much beyond simple logic. In fact, I'm not good at thinking when I'm not working with my hands, which is one reason I like to draw so much.

Drawing helps me think by acting as a guide to the subject of my thoughts. The Jung book sitting on my bedside table reminded me about the subconscious. I think it's the subconscious that I have a dialogue with when I'm drawing. That's why it's so interesting — and hard sometimes — hard because I don't always get past the surface.

I was only in bed thinking a short time that first day of my illness before I had to take up my pen and clipboard with paper and start to draw. The first drawings out of the chute were wimpy things. This changed when I swapped the fountain pen for a calligraphic model with a ragged chisel point. Things happened then — crazy, wild, bloody things. Sparks flew! This was war. Strange thing though, I didn't care. Something had clicked, and I felt a wonderful sense of freedom as I worked, even though the images coming out were chaotic and gruesome.

Right off I decided against passing judgment on subject matter, even though I'd never liked cathartic art, which this was. *So what*, I thought, *this is new territory, and I love new territory.* Then I thought, *Why not let the subject matter wander on its own, but track it, so to speak, by consciously moving one or more elements from one drawing to the next.* By doing this I hoped that a natural continuity from drawing to drawing would be created. I chose the parts of the first drawing I liked, and then moved these into the next drawing and added some new things. I did the same with the next drawing and the next and the next.

Bingo! Through thirty drawings that first day the new approach worked beautifully. Besides that, I loved the ease of access it gave me into the more exotic parts of my mind. I also loved the way it enabled my mind to stop hopping around, wondering where to go, and what to do next. But most of all I was thrilled that such a seemingly insignificant little method, technique, approach, whatever you want to call it, could enhance and expand my creative potential so much, so quickly.

It's over a month old now, my new technique, and I'm still working at it enthusiastically. Drawings continue to peel off the end of my pen easily and naturally, nuance to nuance, one idea to the next. I feel cohesion in my art for the first time — real cohesion. I don't know what this means. Maybe it means that my work will be boring and predictable as long as I work this way. For now though, I'll just savor the moment.

# what we are doing

What we are doing is hard to explain.
It would take diagrams and curse words, complicated
facial expressions
and lengthy descriptions of little-known tools. It would be
like trying to explain *quarks* and *leptons*
to someone who had merely asked
where the restrooms were.

However, to put it simply,
Davey and I
are on the fifth floor of the library, working
partners, jockeying stepladders
back and forth in the narrow aisles between the stacks,
not soaking up knowledge, but Pop-
riveting ceiling grid.

Davey has his ladder, I have mine; each
of us has a small Vise-grips.
From Microbiology to Astrophysics,
dragging our tools and our bodies along with us,
we push on
inexorably, zigzagging
through the Dewey decimal system.

CLEM STARCH

# what we are doing

Pausing for a moment in Immunology,
naturally I think of Holub
peering into his microscope, making a poem
out of lymphocytes!
By the time we reach *The Bella Coola River Estuary*
and *Holocene Carbonate Sedimentation*,
it's noon, and time for lunch.

And cards! The game
has been going on for years,
at least since the time of the Pyramids, if not coeval
with carbonate sedimentation.
Five-card draw, jokers wild. We ante up...
Frank's three queens beat my two pair.
Davey's deal.

The afternoon will be a scorcher.

The participation of married women in the U.S. work force has increased from 20 percent to 60 percent in the last forty years.

. . .

The participation of men in the U.S. work force has decreased from 88 percent to 76 percent in the last forty years.

. . .

As of 1990, 53.7 percent of all American teenagers are holding a job, many of them attending school as well.

*The Overworked American* by Juliet B. Schor, copyright © 1992, BasicBooks, A Division of HarperCollins Publishers, Inc.

TOM HARPOLE

# a matter of degrees

In Fairbanks, Alaska, on January 30, 1989, the air temperature was fifty-six below zero. Ice fog so thickly shrouded the town, I couldn't tell when walking across an intersection if there were cars coming or not. Fan belts, shattered by the cold, kept appearing at my feet as I walked the mile across town the motel owner had warned me not to try. Multiple-car pileups were common. Fairbanks hospitals were treating dozens of ill-clad motorists for frostbite after they had tried to walk for help. The night before, a Canadian military C-130 had crashed while trying to land at Wainwright Army Base, killing eight Canadian soldiers. The crash was blamed on the effects of the record-breaking cold on the Hercules aircraft engines.

When I got to the Sourdough Express Trucking Company, Whitey Gregory, the owner, told me the ride I was supposed to get up the Haul Road to Prudhoe Bay was off. Earlier that day, the Alaska State Department of Transportation had declared the 516-mile all-weather road closed. For the first time in its ten-year history, the remote trail through the Alaska interior was deemed unsafe due to extreme cold.

About then, an average-sized man wearing arctic coveralls walked in from the yard. He pulled off his stocking cap and scarf, revealing features sculpted by high winds: long brown hair combed straight back over the top of his head, a salty auburn beard parted at the chin and swept earward, and a raptor's squint. "My eyebrows froze out there in two minutes," he said. "This weather is appalling."

I was introduced to Clay Gustaves, a 41-year-old driver who was preparing to make an emergency run to Kuparuk oilfield, west of Prudhoe Bay, with a load of deicing methanol. He went back out into the 3:00 P.M. darkness rasping, "Tires." in his Camel smoker voice.

Whitey explained that the DOT agreed to let this one trucker try to haul 8,000 gallons of methanol to the North Slope because the need for it constituted an emergency. None of the Sourdough Express drivers would pull the inflammable load in the prevailing weather conditions, so Gustaves had

69

been contracted to haul it with his independently owned Freightliner. Whitey told me the man has never had an accident in over 900 trips during his nine years plying the Haul Road. He owns the best driving record in the history of the road. His 1983 Freightliner has 660,000 miles on it, all of them earned on the 1,000-mile round trip on the unpaved road from Fairbanks to the oilfields. In this, his last week before he was to take a year off, he wanted all the trips he could get. Whitey said he didn't like the idea of a truck out there alone but figured if anyone could make it, Clay would.

Then he brightened a bit and suggested that if I were willing to risk it, I could ride with Clay. He said if the State DOT objected to a passenger having gone on the trip, he'd smooth things out later. "I'm not trying to talk you into anything, but the road's never been closed before. You'll be the only truck on it. This is a chance to see something unusual."

Clay warned me that during the 500-mile trip north it would only get colder, and that a breakdown could be deadly since there would be no other truckers around to help. If the truck got stuck, but the engine could still run, the heaters in the cab would keep us alive. However, if the extreme cold caused the diesel fuel to gel, or if we hit a moose, or anything else, and damaged the radiator, we'd be stranded without heat. A propane-fueled heater would be useless because at about forty-two below zero, propane freezes. I suggested that if we did have to spend time without the truck's heat, we could just dig a snow cave and wait it out. But Clay told me much of the land north of the Arctic Circle is arctic desert. Even though it is all white up there, the amount of dry snow we'd have to work with wouldn't lend itself readily to caving.

Whitey added another caveat: since aircraft altimeters are calibrated to barometers, and since the record-breaking cold was accompanied by barometric pressure readings that were higher than barometers are commonly built to record, there was no way to calibrate the altimeters; all aircraft in Alaska were grounded for the next few days. There would be no possibility of any rescue by aircraft should we not arrive in Prudhoe Bay when expected. "You will truly be on your own up there," Whitey said.

Gustaves shifted his weight under all his layers of clothing. He was literally bouncing around the office, anxious to get on the road. He said he'd always wanted to drive the only truck in the Arctic. "Make it or not, my friend, this is the real deal. We'll be riding point and cleanup on the northernmost escape from inertia in the world." He slowed down. "It is unimaginably gorgeous up there. All the way." The clarity and promise of that short speech seduced me as if spoken by a wealthy fugitive from a world that strives to eliminate chance.

Despite the urgency about delivering the methanol, we sat five miles north of Fairbanks at the Hilltop truckstop for over an hour while Rosy, the owner, made a sackful of sandwiches and poured coffee. She told us about a film crew from L.A. that had been stranded up near Coldfoot for a few hours the day before. The tame wolves they brought for the film resisted leaving the vans to go out in the cold. When they did set foot out of their cages, they literally tried to stand on one foot at a time. Finally, the story went, the film crew agreed with the wolves' survival instincts, but then none of their vans would start, and they were stranded. A trucker found them several hours later and packed the whole crew into his cab and sleeper and took them to Fairbanks. They had all been flown to Providence Hospital in Anchorage, where they were losing toes to frostbite.

Rosy fretted at Clay while packing our lunches, saying she couldn't believe we were trying this. She gave us extra cookies and fruit and said the oilfields shouldn't need the deicing fluid anyway. The pipeline flow was slowed down because three feet of snow and eighty-mile-per-hour winds at the terminal down at Valdez were preventing oil tankers from sailing. Clay chided Rosy, saying she knew more about the pipeline flow than her own blood pressure. She waved a dishrag in front of her face at nothing, reminded him to buy his three packs of Camels for the trip, and we left.

By 7:00 P.M. the temperature at the weigh station was sixty-seven below zero as we rolled over the scales and weighed in at 99,000 pounds. Clay did a walk-around, thumping all twenty-six tires with a billy club while listening for any variations in the dull thuds. He tapped the tank once and said he likes hauling fluids. The tank trailers have internal baffles, but the surging and splashing back there still goes on and adds another dimension to the job. A "wet" load becomes a live influence on a trip up the Haul Road.

The road north from Fairbanks to Livengood is officially called the Elliot Highway. Haul Road truckers call the first forty miles Moose Alley. Moose tracks pock the snow-packed surface. Moose prefer walking the smooth road to weaving through the dense, scrubby white spruce and alder woods that crowd the roads. Snow-removal crews blade down the berm of plowed snow at the road's edge so the moose can get off the road when trucks are using it. We saw several. They magnificently ignored us.

At 62 Mile, near Livengood, the rubber seal on my door had shrunk from the cold enough to allow the door to pop open. We stopped, and Clay used some "100-mile-per-hour-tape" (duct tape) to connect a piece of heater hose to the defroster. After blowing warm air on the seal for half an hour, the door would stay shut. "Victory is mine, sayeth Clayborn," he announced. "Any trip on the Haul Road is more of a project than a drive." He advised me not to use my door unless I had to jump.

In a few miles, we came to the first 16 percent grade (passenger car roads never exceed 8 percent). Clay told me to grab my coat and be ready to jump. If the wheels start to slip on a steep grade, the truck can "spin out," lose momentum, and stop. The warm tires immediately turn the snowpacked surface to ice, and the truck will slide backward uncontrollably. If that happened we would both have to jump and hope the truck wasn't wrecked. "The trick to jumping properly," Clay coached me, "is to jump pretty far out there so you don't slide back under the truck. Make it a good jump."

After several more hills like that, hills on which we kept coats on our laps and a grip on our door handles, Clay stopped at the top of Hess hill to relax. "Take charge a little," he called it. Walking around the truck, we found the first shattered tire. Jagged edges showed where shards of tread and sidewall rubber, bigger than a handprint, had cracked off. Clay said he'd never seen a tire shatter like that. It was fifty miles to the Yukon Bridge truckstop, where we could repair or replace it.

By 11:30 P.M., we'd made the first 150 miles and reached the Yukon River Bridge. Toby Williams, sixty-five, the manager of Yukon Bridge Ventures, was in his shop but was surprised there was a truck on the Haul Road this night. Toby has a bad back, and he had no hired help on hand. We now had three shattered tires to replace, and Clay also discovered that the main U-joint to the drive axles was loose. There were no replacement U-joints big enough to fit the Freightliner at Yukon Bridge, but Clay decided we could make it to Coldfoot and see if they had one. We changed the shattered tires in a series of ten-minute efforts that weren't physically exhausting but left us breathless from trying to get the job done without sucking in much of the arctic air. The twin chrome exhaust stacks pushed diesel plumes hard at the crystallized air. The interface, where fumes met ice fog, looked as plainly drawn as two hot-air balloons inflating.

While the truck idled at Yukon Bridge, the gear lube in the transmissions and differential almost solidified. When we got the load moving again, the U-joint held. It withstood the engine's tremendous torque and the resistance of the frozen lubricants clotting the drive train. As we drove back onto the road again, the gear shifts were nearly impossible for Clay to manipulate. He drove for six or seven miles at a crawl to allow the lubricants to warm up. During our deliberate ascent up the three-mile hill called the Beaverslide, he put his hand to his left ear as though listening to something gone wrong and said, "Oh no, why didn't I check it back at

Yukon Bridge? There's no turning back now." I involuntarily grabbed my coat as I tried to hear the problem. But his concern was for the clasp for his diamond earring that had fallen off while changing tires. "Personal rigging losses on the tough old Haul Road," he laughed.

In the relative quiet of the slow going up Beaverslide, he told me that some truckers won't stop at Yukon Bridge because the word is out that a religious cult bought the place. But he thinks that living at that outpost will keep them humble. He talked about his father teaching him to drive big rigs in a log truck in Idaho twenty-five years ago — the same truck that killed his dad. Now he believes his father watches over him, keeping him safe. We both spoke of fathers prematurely dead, and our ongoing faith in their protective powers that has let us both be strangely tempted by abnormal doings.

At about 6:00 A.M. a Fairbanks radio station announced it was seventy-fou below zero there. The state of emergency declared by the governor was still in effect. All records for low temperatures in Alaska had been broken. The announcer also asked that all nonessential workers voluntarily stay home. "How would you like to decide for yourself that you're nonessential?" Clay wondered, as the fifty-ton load he was causing to move through the arctic began to limber up and live again.

Farther down the road, after driving along the narrow spine of the Kanuti Mountains for thirty-five miles, we crossed the Arctic Circle. At that moment we were listening a tape of Robin Williams' explanation of how God designed the platypus. Between the Arctic Circle and Stormy Hill, the Northern Lights began to wash greens and golds across the entire sky. Under the ethereal glow we drove by a trailer loaded with structural steel, abandoned on the side of the road. It was the first of several forsaken loads we would pass on the way to the North Slope. Clay said the poor soul hauling that load just unhooked it a few days ago, drove back to Fairbanks bobtail, and quit. He talked about drivers killed or just psychologically wrecked by the Haul Road as we drove through Bonanza Creek over hundreds of fresh moose tracks. He said that for the last fifty miles we had been driving on top of four or five feet of accumulated ice and snow. "This road works on extremes," he said. "It builds up, and you think the jackpot is getting bigger. Then these drivers decide for themselves that the loads are all millstones, and it's all tragedy instead." He held me with a look that kept his eyes off the road for a couple of seconds.

As we drove along, most of our conversations were short and yelled. Talk happened as an adjunct to his occupation. He never looked away from the road, and he was never idle. The steering wheel is as big as the top of a cock-tail-lounge table, and about as horizontal. He constantly corrected our course, riding with most of his torso bent over the big wheel like a jockey on a whale. Clay wasn't just driving; he was using all his limbs, his extremities, like a wizened athlete competing in a game in which the rules can change instantly. At its roomiest, the road gives drivers thirty-two feet of width to work with. We had already seen dozens of places in the roadside berms where a driver had deviated a few feet and plowed into the ditch. After failing to plumb the mysteries of the transmissions, I did try to keep track of how many times he changed gears. By the end of our run to the North Slope, I estimated that in the 516-mile trip he shifted gears over 1,800 times.

The all-weather road, from the Yukon River to Prudhoe Bay, was built in one year. It demands the upper limits of diesel tractor capabilities as well as mighty levels of human skill. Theoretically, it is always possible to pull a load on it without using tire chains. But the contingencies crop up and are mortally threatening. The road, where it steepened, was rutted and gouged from many recent spinouts. Clay dropped down a gear and steered the truck right out to the edge of the ruts and tracks and then a bit farther, where the snow was virgin and traction might be better. "If this doesn't work, I'll be wanting to jump out your side," he barked. Just out his door was an abysmal drop into darkness. The eight drive tires caught and Clay finished the hill without needing to downshift. At the summit, he stopped and we got out. He didn't bother with his coat, but stomped around silently on the verge of the road, cigarette sticking from the dead center of his parted beard. He blew gouts of smoke as he looked down at the narrow edge he'd just used to make it up the hill. Then he declared he loves, just loves, this job. He can't believe they pay him to live such a life.

We found two more shattered tires on the trailer up there. When we got back in the cab, I asked what were the chances we'd break a front tire. "Chances are," he said. "Then what?" I asked. Clay said he'd probably be trying to steer right up to the point we wrecked. There are twenty-four wheels on the truck that can only go straight. If you lose one of the two that steer, you can't control anything with 99,000 pounds pushing you where it will. He said he hoped I wasn't scared.

I thought back to ten years of timber-falling and using explosives during my logging career in the Pacific Northwest, and about how seldom fear had ever helped. But a person still worries.

We reached Coldfoot by 9:00 A.M. and were met by Dick Mackey, who won the 1,049-mile-long Iditarod sled-dog race in 1978. He and his wife, Cathy, put the winnings down to start the "Northernmost Truckstop in the

World," as his hat says. A school bus with a plywood shed attached served as the first cafe. Ten years later they have an airstrip, a truck repair shop, a 100-seat cafe, a real home, and 160 beds in refurbished pipeline buildings that they bought cheap and hauled to Coldfoot. The energy bill for their businesses now runs about $125,000 per year. The entire operation at Coldfoot is a fossil-fuel-based microcosm. It's the midway-point between Fairbanks and Prudhoe Bay, the last place on the road to buy necessities. They don't sell gasoline. There has never been a call for car fuel that far north.

Dick took me and my steaming cup of coffee out in the parking lot for my "Cheechako Initiation." He told me to throw the coffee up in the air. I did, and heard some soft popping and cracking sounds, like a whole bowl of Rice Krispies going off at once. A tan cloud of flash-frozen coffee crystals drifted away. Not a drop made it to the ground. The thermometer on the outside of the cafe read seventy-nine below zero.

When we changed the shattered tires, we broke two big lug wrenches. The steel snapped easily after the wrenches had been out in the cold for more than a few minutes. There are design factors that account for cold weather, that are incorporated into the manufacture of rubber, metals, fuels, coffee, and people too, for that matter. But all the design criteria for making things that are useful where humans can live and work had no sway over the winter of 1989 in the Arctic. Eighty degrees below zero is ruinously cold.

By 11:00 A.M. indirect sunlight was competing with the goldfish-pink glow from the parking-lot lights. The shattered tires were changed, and since we couldn't get a replacement U-joint, Clay welded the loose one solid. We drove away slowly to see if anything was going to break.

The tincture of sunrise suffusing the tops of the Endicott Mountains to the west tailgated us for the next few hours. Just before we crossed a bridge at the north end of the Dietrich Valley, we stopped to look at an overturned tractor and trailerload of pipe about fifty yards down from the road. "This is an unforgiving corner." Clay said. I wanted to photograph the scene in the soft light, so I framed a few shots with wreckage foreground, pipeline middleground, and Brooks Range background. When I climbed back into the cab Clay was playing a rock and roll tape. It was Omar and the Howlers doing "Hard Times in the Land of Plenty." Clay estimated that righting the wreck and towing fees to Fairbanks would cost about $14,000.

By 1:00 P.M. we were eighty miles north of Coldfoot on the Chandalar Shelf. The road led to a high valley cleft under dozens of unnamed peaks.

Atigun Pass loomed ahead as the valley narrowed and we rolled along next to the pipeline. The 6,800-foot pass posed one of the greatest challenges to pipeline and road construction in the entire 800-mile length of the corridor. But it is the path of least resistance through the Brooks Range, where 8,000-foot peaks rising from near sea level are the rule. In the twilight, seen from below, its steepness and length looked impossible. Clay called it the granddaddy truck eater of them all and figured he has seen about 200 wrecks on Atigun Pass. A sign at the foot says, "Avalanches Next 44 Miles." Clay told me about spending three days in his sleeper when a series of three avalanches partially buried his truck a few weeks before. The first one stopped him and blocked the road, so he climbed back into his sleeper and was awakened by a second that pushed his truck towards the edge of the road. The third buried most of the cab and jammed the whole outfit against the guardrail. He dug a breather hole for the air-cleaner canister on the side of the truck, restarted the engine, and read Larry McMurtry's *Lonesome Dove* for three days until help arrived. He told me, "If we spin out, try to jump out my door." If I were to jump out my side, he said, I could fall 600 feet or more. The guardrail had been replaced a couple months before, but in the first seven or eight miles of the ascent, it had already been bent, scraped, or torn away completely.

At the summit of Atigun Pass, Clay Gustaves exulted, "This is it, the top of my world. It's all downhill from here." The top of his world is pure white and true blue. Two ravens casually kept pace just outside our windows, waiting for scraps of food, their black beaks opened and closed noiselessly. He downshifted and we descended the arctic slope of the Brooks Range to the sweeping steppes and plains that drain to the Beaufort Sea, some 150 miles north.

From twenty miles south of Prudhoe Bay, the immensity of the oilfields is staggering. A thirty-five-mile-long sprawl of lights defines the 900 wells, major facilities, airports, and many roads. It looks like a city. The Prudhoe Bay oilfields have cost more than $20 billion to develop. They comprise the biggest oil production facility in North America. Clay turned on the radio to listen to the broadcast from Point Barrow, some 170 miles to the west of Prudhoe Bay. The announcer was speaking in Eskimo, introducing golden oldies from the fifties.

On that last stretch of road, Clay talked about his forthcoming year off. He is going to ship his Harley to his dad's shop in Idaho and spend a month or so rebuilding it. He will paint it "Two-Click Red." I asked him to describe that shade and he looked at me archly. "The color of those red shoes that take Dorothy home in *The Wizard of Oz*," he said. Once he fixes her up, Clay wants to ride the old cream puff to warm places. He thinks a year on paved roads will make him lonely for the Arctic. He told me I had just seen one of his favorite trips ever on the Haul Road. During the twenty-three-hour trip the average temperature had been seventy-three below zero. He was already calling on his C.B., arranging to do some "hosteling." He intended to drop this load, turn right back, and begin pulling those half-dozen loads we saw abandoned to their intended destinations.

I talked him into joining me at the Deadhorse Motel for supper before he went back down the road. Over lobster thermidor we talked of all-time engineering accomplishments such as the pyramids, Hoover Dam, and others. We agreed that the Haul Road and pipeline demand admiration on their own merits as unparalleled feats of engineering. Clay told me there is a monument down in Valdez to commemorate the completion of the pipeline and road. The plaque reads, "We didn't know it couldn't be done." He said that is a cliché up here anymore, but it's still the theme. Then he headed back out to his idling Freightliner.

About a month after I returned from Alaska, news of the oil spill in Prince William Sound intruded like a blizzard on Easter weekend. I phoned a number of Alaskans I had met during my travels to hear their reactions. Feelings ran from dismay to outrage. For many workers up there, life is risky, but despite long odds against them, a frontier spirit pervades and the jobs get done. Now a sense of betrayal or defeat seemed to have traumatized those I spoke with. Alaskans are in mourning.

After making a few phone calls, I located Clay Gustaves in Idaho, where he was vacationing. I wanted to know how he felt about the oil spill. "Appalling," he said. "We've been working towards a tragedy for ten years without admitting it." He slowed down. "It is the sure and final loss of innocence for Alaska." He spoke of the 900 trips he made from Fairbanks up the Pipeline Haul Road to the North Slope. He is proud of never having wrecked a truck, prouder still of never hitting or injuring a moose or caribou. Like many Alaskans engaged in dangerous tasks of extraction, whether fishing, mining, logging, or producing oil, Clay has taken care to do things properly. "I loved the demands of that kind of driving, and it made me rich. I loved the risks, the excitement. I love the Arctic," he said. "It was like a jackpot just getting bigger all the time, but none of us let ourselves think it could turn tragic so fast." There was a very long pause. "I won't partake any more," he said. "I was only going to take a year off, but now I swear I'm not going back."

# "girl" on the crew

The boys flap heavy leather aprons at me
like housewives scaring crows
from the clean back wash.
        Some aprons.        Some wash.
They think if the leather is tough enough
if the hammer handle piercing it is long enough
I will be overcome with primordial dread
or longing.

They chant construction curses at me:
        *Lay 'er down! Erect those studs!*
and are alarmed when I learn the words.
They build finely tuned traps, give orders I cannot fill
then puzzle when a few of their own
give me passwords.

I learn the signs of entry,
dropping my hammer into its familiar mouth
as my apron whispers *O-o-o-h Welcome!*

I point my finger and corner posts spring into place
shivering themselves into fertile earth at my command.
The surveyors have never seen such accuracy.

I bite off nails with my teeth
shorten boards with a wave of my hand
pierce them through the dark brown love knots.
They gasp.

# "girl" on the crew

I squat and the flood of my urine digs
whole drainage systems in an instant.
The boys park their backhoes, call their friends
to come see for themselves or they'd never believe it.

The hairs of my head turn to steel and join boards
tongue-in-groove
like lovers along dark lanes.
Drywall is rustling under cover
eager to slip over the studs at my desire.

When I tire, my breasts grow two cherry trees
that depart my chest
and offer me shade, cool juices
while the others suck bitter beans.

At the end of the day the boys are exhausted
from watching.
They fall at my feet and beg for a body like mine.
I am too busy dancing to notice.

KATE BRAID

# the female form

He called me "Carpenteress,"
that kid in the white T-shirt
with a pack of Players rolled in his sleeve.

A form of deference, no doubt.
I would prefer he kissed
my steel-toed boot.

I do the work of men
around me, but they are honored
by their title, Carpenter.

What's the difference? Ah, I know!
he must have noticed my boots where
the leather at the toe, scrapped
across too many plywood floors as I knelt
reveals bare metal underneath —
the open-toed look for summer!

Perhaps he picked up on the classic lines
of my plaid shirt? Fifty
cents at my couturier, the Sally Ann
a foreign store in these wealthy parts of town.

KATE BRAID

# the female form

Did he notice the touch of color at my neck
where the inhalator drapes softly
from black rubber straps
leaving two dark marks — carpenter's blush —
carved on my cheeks?

No? Then it was
the turn of my curls set off nicely
by the pert yellow hard hat.
He noted the cheerful line
of the upturned brim, also useful
for shedding rain.

But of course, it was the gloves I wear
for unloading lumber trucks,
this season's bulky look,
squared off, casual, in blue
the color of my eyes
accented with mud.

It's that look of the great outdoors
so natural, the Carpenteress,
doing the work of Men
with that special fashion flair.

# words of work

### CAN OPENER ARTIST
A logger's term for a poor cook.

### ANTIGODLIN'
A logger's term for being off line or off the track.

### CLAM DIGGER
In coastal logging camps, a no-good logger.

### GANDY DANCER
A section hand working on the construction of a railroad.

### GRAPE PICKER
A logger's term for a worker who shines up to the boss whenever possible.

### GRAB THE SNOTTY END
A logger's term for taking the heaviest end of a job.

### HALF-NELSON ON THE PAYROLL
A logger with relatives among the company bosses.

*Woods Words*, by Walter F. McCulloch, copyright 1958, Oregon Historical Society and Champoeg Press.

NORMAN MACLEAN

# smokejumpers

Nearly every jumper fears this moment. If he continues to miss sleep because of it, he doesn't tell anybody but he quits the Smokejumpers and joins up with something like the crew that makes trails. Whatever he tries, it is something close to the ground, and he never tries jumping again because it makes him vomit.

Fear could be part of the reason they were jumping only fifteen men on this day — one had become sick on the flight over. Although he was an experienced jumper, his repressions had caught up with him and he had become ill on each of his flights this season and had not been able to jump. This was a rough trip, and after he had vomited and crawled out of it and his jump suit, he must have made his decision. When he landed back in Missoula, he resigned from the Smokejumpers.

It was a record temperature outside and the air was turbulent, so much so that Sallee once told me that they were all half sick and trying to be in the first stick to jump and get on the ground. But, weather aside, it was hard to know on what day this or that good man had built up more anxiety than he could handle, and at the last minute on this day this crew of fifteen was jumping four sticks of 4-4-4-3. On the ground, however, the crew was to pick up another firefighter who had been fighting the fire alone, so when the showdown came the crew was again sixteen.

The fear of the jumpers is a complicated matter, because in some ways a part of each of them is not afraid. Most of them, for instance, believe that God is out there, or a spirit or a something in the sky that holds them up. "You wouldn't dare jump," they say, "if it was empty out there." Also they say, "Why be afraid? You are jumping in a parachute, and the government made the parachute, didn't it?" This is connected with their thinking that guys who hang glide from the tops of the big mountains surrounding

From the book *Young Men And Fire* by Norman Maclean © 1992 by The University of Chicago. Published with permission from The University of Chicago Press.

Missoula are crazy. "They're crazy," the Smokejumpers say. "They don't have a government parachute." So in some strange way they think they are jumping on the wings of God and the government. This does not keep them from worrying some nights — maybe every night — before they jump, and it does not keep some of them from vomiting as they are about to jump.

Understandably, Smokejumpers have an obsession about their equipment. Although they change from one fixation to another, equipment is nearly always somewhere on their mind, and, as they get close to the jump, equipment is about all that is on their mind. They know they are about to live or die on a man-made substitute for wings furnished by the government. They start saying to themselves, as if it had never occurred to them before, "What the hell does the government know about making a parachute that will open five seconds after it starts to fall? Not a damn thing. They just farm it out to some fly-by-night outfit that makes the lowest bid." As the jump nears, their general fears focus on what seems the least substantial and the most critical piece of their equipment — the static line that is supposed to jerk the parachute open with a *woof* twelve feet after it drops from the plane.

The attention the jumper has to pay to the elaborate and studied ritual of jumping helps to keep his fears manageable. He stands by the spotter lying on the left of the door, who holds the jumper by the left foot. The next signs are by touch and not by word — the whole flight is made with the door open, unless it is going to be a very long one, so words can't be trusted in the roar of the wind. Using the sill of the open door as a gunsight, the spotter waits for the landing area to appear in it and next allows for the wind drift. The spotter then says "Go," or something like that, but the jumper doesn't step into the sky until he feels the tap on the calf of his left leg, and in his dreams he remembers the tap. With the tap he steps into the sky left foot first so that the wind drift will not throw him face-first into the plane's tail just to his left. He leaves for earth in the "tuck position," a position somewhat like the one he was in before he was born. This whole business of appearing on earth from the sky has several likenesses to nativity.

The jumpers are forced into this crouched, prenatal moment almost by the frame of things. The jumper, unlike the hang glider, is not up there for scenic purposes. He comes closer to plummeting than to gliding. He is to land as close as possible to the target the spotter has picked, and all the jumpers are supposed to do the same so no time will be lost in collecting and piling their stuff in the same pile and being off to the fire. In order to drop as straight as possible, the jumpers originally would stand straight up in front of the door of the plane and the spotter would say, "Do you see the jump spot down there?" But if the jumper was a new man, the spotter wouldn't look to see if the jumper was seeing. He knew the jumper would be standing rigid with his eyes squeezed shut, looking as if he were looking at the distant horizon. But the spotter, needing to be sure that at least he was heard, would ask again, "Do you see the jump spot down there?" And the new jumper, frozen on the horizon, would say, "Yes, sir." Then he would get the tap on the left leg, but before he could jump he had to crouch in the tuck position because the favorite plane of the early Smokejumpers was the Ford TriMotor that had just a small opening for a door. So it was more or less the frame of things that forced a Smokejumper to be born again as he jumped.

His whole flight to the ground takes an average of only a minute. This minute is about the only moment a Smokejumper is ever alone, and it is one of the most lonely moments in his life. A Smokejumper never is sent alone to a fire; the minimum number is two; at their base Smokejumpers live in their dormitory with roommates or, if they live in Missoula, with their families; at night they are with their girls and often with other Smokejumpers who are with their girls, and if they get into a fight at a bar they are immediately supported by these other Smokejumpers. For the eternity of this one minute Smokejumpers are alone. It is not that they lose faith in God for that moment. It is just that He is not there anymore or anywhere else. Nothing is there except the jumper and his equipment made by the lowest bidder, and he himself has thinned out to the vanishing point of being only decisions once made that he can't do anything about ever after.

The moment the jumper starts falling is umbilical; he starts by counting, putting "one thousand" in front of each number to slow each count to a second. If he gets to "one thousand five," he knows he is in trouble and pulls the handle that releases the emergency chute on his chest. If, however, his umbilical relation to the plane is properly severed by his twelve-foot static line, his regular parachute explodes, the *woof* vibrates in the rocks below, and his feet are thrown over his head. So it is to be born in the sky — with a loud noise and your feet where your head ought to be. So it is to be born in the sky with a loud noise — the moment you cease to be umbilical you become seed, blown by the wind. It is very lonely for a young man to be seed in the wind. Although you are seed, the sky still seems like the womb and you as seed are blown around the sky's interior parts until you light on the top of a tree or hard rocks or grass, the grass often being only a cover for hard rocks. If you land on the top of a tree, you are probably lucky, especially if you have a long rope in your pocket by which you can let yourself down to the rocks — but only a small percentage when they touch earth land on the tops of trees. Try as they may to avoid landing on rocks, many do. Landing smoothly from the sky does not come naturally to man.

As in life generally, it is most common to land in grass that thinly covers very hard rocks. If a jumper lands on flat ground at all, it is something like jumping off the roof of an automobile going twenty-five miles an hour, and in 1949 he finished his jump by taking the "Allen roll," landing sideways, with the right side from the hip down taking the shock, the upper part of the body continuing to pivot to the right until the body falls on its back and then rolls over on its knees. As a jumping instructor once said, the roll is to spread the pain all over the body.

So it is to appear on the earth from the sky. It is not surprising, considering the punishment the jumper takes at both ends of the jump, that no big man can be a Smokejumper, and we have to remind ourselves from time to time that, although we keep saying "men," most of them are still close to boys and that they are not very big boys. Most of the seventeen or eighteen thousand visitors a year at the Smokejumper base in Missoula, having heard, possibly from the Smokejumpers themselves, that the Smokejumpers are the Forest Service's best, expect to see the Minnesota Vikings professional football team practicing outside their dormitory, but instead they see teams of fairly ordinary-looking boys playing volleyball, their sizes ranging from five feet four to six feet two, with a maximum weight in 1949 of 190 pounds. The name of the game is not important to Smokejumpers. The competition is. In the Smokejumpers they don't recruit losers or big men, who don't seem to be made to drop out of the sky.

This was a fairly rough landing. Sallee lit in a lodgepole, his feet just off the ground, but none of the rest of them were lucky enough to break their fall. They rolled through rocks, although only Dodge was injured. Hellman and Rumsey came to help him and found him with an elbow cut to white bone, the cut somehow self-sealed so that it did not bleed. They bandaged the elbow, and Dodge said only that it was stiff, and the next day he said only that it was stiffer.

They crawled out of their jump suits that made them look part spacemen and part football players. In 1949 they even wore regular leather football helmets; then there was wire mesh over their faces, the padded canvas suit (with damn little padding), and logger boots. They tagged their jump suits and stacked them in one pile. Their work clothes, unlike their jump suits, were their own, and they were mostly just ordinary work clothes — Levis and blue shirts, but hard hats. None in this crew appeared in white shirts and oxfords, although Smokejumpers have appeared on fires in their drinking clothes when there has been an emergency call and they have been picked up in a bar, and a jumper is quite a sight in a white shirt and oxfords after he has been on a fire for three or four days and had a hangover to start with.

87

Then the plane began to circle, dropping cargo. It was being dropped high and was scattering all over the head of the gulch. Because the cargo had been dropped at two thousand feet instead of the customary twelve hundred so the pilot would not have to take his plane close to the ridgetops in the heavy winds, the men had to collect the cargo over at least a three-hundred-square-yard area. In those days the bedrolls were dropped without benefit of parachutes and popped all over the landscape, some of them bouncing half as high as the trees. The parachutes were made of nylon because grasshoppers like the taste of silk. In a modern tragedy you have to watch out for little details rather than big flaws. By the end, every minute would count, but it took the crew some extra minutes to collect the cargo because it was so scattered. Suddenly there was a terrific crash about a quarter of a mile down the canyon from the landing area. It turned out to be the radio, whose parachute hadn't opened because its static line had broken where it was attached to the plane. Another detail. The pulverized radio, which had fallen straight, told the crew about how far downgulch from the landing area they had been jumped, so the spotter must have been allowing for about a quarter of a mile of wind drift. It also told them something else — that the outside world had disappeared. The only world had become Mann Gulch and a fire, and the two were soon to become one and the same and never to be separated, at least in story.

They finished collecting and piling up their cargo. Dodge estimated that the crew and cargo were dropped by 4:10 P.M. but that it was nearly 5:00 before all the cargo had been retrieved.

Dodge made the double L signal on the landing area with orange sleeves, signaling to the plane, all present and accounted for. The plane circled twice to be sure and then headed for the outside world. It headed straight down Mann Gulch and across the glare of the Missouri. It seemed to be leaving frighteningly fast, and it was. It had started out a freight train, loaded with cargo. Now it was light and fast and was gone. Its departure left the world much smaller.

There was nothing in the universe now but the terminal glare of the Missouri, an amphitheater of stone erected by geology, and a sixty-acre fire with a future. Whatever the future, it was all to take place here, and soon. Of the Smokejumpers' three elements, sky had already changed to earth. In about an hour the earth and even the sky would all be fire.

# overstory: zero

## THE MAIN THING

The main thing is to have a big breakfast. It's not any easy thing to do at 4 A.M., but it is essential because lunch won't come for another seven or eight hours and there's four or more hours of grueling work to do before you can sit down and open up your lunch box.

The kids on the crew, eighteen-year-olds fresh out of school, sleep in the extra half-hour and don't eat until the morning store stop on the way out to the unit. They wolf down a Perky Pie, a candy bar, and a can of soda in the crummy. They go through the brush like a gut-shot cat for awhile and then drag ass for the rest of the morning. But if you're an old-timer, in your mid-twenties, you know how to pace yourself for the long haul.

You're exhausted, of course, and your calves, hips, arms, and lower back are stiff and sore. But you're used to that. You're always tired and hurting. The only time you feel normal is when you're on the slopes, when the stiffness and fatigue are melted off by the work. It gets worse every morning until by Saturday it takes hours to feel comfortable on a day off. Sunday morning you wake up at four o'clock, wide awake and ready to stomp through downtown Tokyo breathing fire and scattering tanks with your tail.

Your stomach is queasy but you force the good food into it anyway, a big stack of pancakes with peanut butter and syrup, four eggs, bacon, and coffee. There is a point when your belly refuses to take any more. Saliva floods your mouth and you force back the retching, put the forkful of food down on the plate and light another cigarette.

It's dark outside and it's raining, of course. They aren't called the Cascades for nothing. It's December and the solstice sun won't rise until eight, three hours and a hundred miles from home, somewhere along a logging road upriver.

Raincoat and rain pants, hard hat, rubber work gloves, cotton liner gloves, and a stiff pair of caulk boots stuffed with newspaper crowd around the woodburner. All the gear is streaked with mud except the boots, which are caked with an inch-thick mud sole covering the steel spikes. The liner gloves hang stiff and brown, the curving fingers frozen, like a dismembered manikin's hand making an elegant but meaningless gesture.

Mornings are slow. It's hard to move quickly when your stomach is bloated, your body is stiff, and, despite the coffee, your mind is still fatigue-foggy. You have to move though, or miss your ride and lose your job. You try an experimental belch, which doesn't bring up too much half-chewed food and relieves the pressure.

The laxative effect of the coffee would send you to the toilet, but your ride to town is due soon, so you save it for later. Better to shit on company time anyway, squatting out in the brush. It gives you a pleasant break, a few minutes of privacy, and it pisses off Jimboy, the foreman, since, being a college boy and therefore trained to worry about what people think of him, he could never bring himself to actually complain about it.

Lester the Rat taught him that lesson the first week of the season. Les planted a seedling and straightened up and turned his back on the slope to empty his bladder. The foreman glanced back to see him standing there with his back turned, staring idly across to the opposite slope.

"Hey, Gaines, get back to work! Let's go!"

The Rat turned to face him and shook the last golden drops off. He smiled pleasantly, showing a mouth full of crooked snoose-stained teeth. "Sure thing Jim," he said mildly, "You bet." None of the professors up at the university had ever mentioned anything like that, and Jimboy blushed delicately while all up and down the line the crew snickered.

Jimboy makes more money than you do and doesn't work as hard, which is bad enough. But he's also afraid. It's his first winter on the slopes, and he's not used to riding herd on a gang of brush apes. He also wants to make a good impression on his boss, the head forester, so he tries to push his ten-man crew into ever-greater production. He sees himself as a leader of men, a rugged scientist overseeing the great work of industrial progress.

Everyone tries to get his goat so that, with any luck, he'll amuse us some day by breaking out in tears like Tommyboy, the last foreman, did. "You guys are just animals," Tommyboy sobbed, setting off a delighted chorus of wolf howls and coyote yelps. It was the high point of the season and a considerable source of pride for the whole crew.

## CRUMMY TIME

The mercury arc lamps light up the mill with a weird, hellish orange glow. Steam rises from the boilers and there's a sour rotting smell everywhere.

The huge metal buildings bristle with an improbable looking tangle of chains and belts and pipes. There's a constant whistling, clanging, and screaming coming from them.

Through the huge open doorways you can see the mill hands at work in their T-shirts, sorting out an unending river of lumber and veneer like desperate dwarves. They make more money than you and stay dry, but you feel pity and contempt for them. The poor bastards stand in one spot all night, moving to the computerized rhythm of conveyors instead of their own human speed. The cavernous interior of the mill seems as cramped as a closet compared to the slopes.

You work for the mill but not in the mill, on a company reforestation crew. Most of the company land is planted by contractors, but the mill runs a crew that plants land that they won't touch — too steep or too ravaged or too brushy for them.

Acres away, beyond the log pond, past the tall walls of stacked logs, next to the hangar-sized heavy equipment repair shop, is a small refrigerated trailer full of seedling trees in large waxed boxes. Mudflap and Sluggo are helping Jimboy load tree boxes into the back of a four-wheel-drive crew-cab pickup. They are young, straight out of high school, and eager to get a promised job in the mill come spring — if they "work hard and show up every day," of course.

You transfer your gear over to a mud-covered Chevy Suburban crummy. The rig is a mess, both outside and inside. The seats are torn, the headliner is gone, the ceiling drips from the condensed breath of its packed occupants. But you have a great fondness for the ugly thing. It is an oasis of comfort compared to the slopes.

We spend a large part of our lives roaring up and down river powered by its monster 454 V-8. None of this crummy time is paid time. Only the forty hours per week on the slopes earns us money. The other ten to twenty hours of tedium are not the company's concern. Together with the half-hour lunch, we spend eleven to thirteen hours a day together for our eight hours' pay.

All winter long we see each other more than we see our wives and children. We know each other intimately after so many cramped hours. We bicker and tease each other halfheartedly, like an old bitter couple, out of habit more than need.

## ARITHMETIC

The ten of us plant about 7,000 seedling trees every day, enough for each planter to cover a little over an acre of logged-off mountainside. It gets depressing when you start adding it up: 700 per day=3,500 per week=14,000 per month=56,000 trees in a season for one man planting one tree at a time.

Maybe you've seen the TV commercials put out by the company: panoramas of snowcapped mountains, silvery lakes and rivers, closeups of cute critters frolicking, young stands of second growth all green and even as a manicured lawn, and a square-jawed handsome woodsman tenderly planting a seedling. The commercials make reforestation seem heartwarming, wholesome, and benevolent, like watching a Disney flick where a scroungy mutt plays the role of a wild coyote.

Get out a calculator and start figuring it: 700 trees in eight hours=87.5 trees per hour, or 1.458 trees per minute — one punched in every forty-one seconds. How much tenderness can you give a small green seedling in forty-one seconds?

Planting is done with an improbable looking tool called a hoedag. Imagine a heavy metal plate fourteen inches long and four inches wide, maybe five pounds of steel, mounted on a single-bit axe handle. Two or three sideways hacking strokes scalp a foot-square patch of ground, three or four stabs with the tip and the blade is buried up to the haft. Six blows 700 times=4,200 per day. At five pounds each, that comes to 21,000 pounds of lifting. Generally, what's left of the topsoil isn't deep enough to sink a 'dag in, so you punch through whatever subsoil, rocks, or roots lie hidden by the veneer of dirt.

You pump up and down on the handle, break up the soil, open a hole, dangle the roots down there, and pull the blade out. The dirt pulls the roots down to the bottom of the hole, maybe ten or tewlve inches deep. You give it a tug to pull the root collar even with the ground and tamp the soil around it with your foot.

The next tree goes in eight feet away from the last one and eight feet from the next man in line's tree. Two steps and you're there. It's a sort of rigorous dance, all day long — scalp, stab, stuff, stomp, and split; scalp, stab, stuff, stomp, and split — every forty-one seconds or less, 700 or more times a day.

Seven hundred trees eight feet apart comes to a line of seedlings 5,600 feet long — a mile and some change. Of course, the ground is never level. You march up and down mountains all day — straight up and straight down, since, although nature never made a straight line, forestry professors and their students are fond of them. So you climb a quarter-mile straight down and then back up, eat lunch, and do it again.

The ground itself is never really clear, even on the most carefully charred reforestation unit. Stumps, old logs, debris, boulders, and brush have to be gone over or through or around with almost every step. Two watertight tree bags, about the size and shape of brown paper grocery bags, hang on your hips, rubbing them raw under the weight of the thirty to forty pounds of seedlings stuffed inside them.

It's best not to think about it all. The proper attitude is to consider yourself as eternally damned, with no tomorrow or yesterday — just the unavoidable present to endure. Besides, you tell yourself, it's not so bad once you get used to it.

## OUTLAWS

Tree planting is done by winos and wetbacks, hillbillies and hippies for the most part. It is brutal, mind-numbing, underpaid stoop labor. Down there in Hades, Sisyphus sees the tree planters and thanks his lucky star because he's got such a soft gig.

Being at the bottom of the Northwest social order and the top of the local ass-busting order gives you an exaggerated pride in what you do. You invade a small grocery store like a biker gang. It's easy to mistake fear for higher forms of respect, and as a planter you might as well.

In a once-rugged society gone docile, you have inherited a vanishing tradition of ornery individualism. The ghosts of drunken bullwhackers, miners, rowdy cowpunchers, and bomb-tossing Wobblies count on you to keep alive the 120-proof spirit of irreverence towards civilization that built the West.

A good foreman, one who rises from the crew by virtue of outworking everybody else, understands this and uses it to build his crew and drive them to gladly work harder than necessary. A foreman who is uncomfortable with the underlying violence of his crew becomes its target. It is rare for a crew to actually beat up a foreman, but it happens.

## BAG-UP

The long, smelly ride ends on a torn-up moonscape of gravel. No one stirs. You look out the foggy windows of the crummy through a gray mist of Oregon dew at the unit. You wonder what shape it's in, how steep, how brushy, how rocky; red sticky clay or yellow doughy clay; freshly cut or decades old; a partial replanting or a first attempt. The answers lie hidden behind a curtain of rain, and you're not eager to find out.

The foreman steps out and with a few mutterings the crummies empty. Ten men jostle for their equipment in the back of the crummies. Most planters aren't particular about which tree bag they use, but each man has a favorite 'dag that is rightfully his. A greenhorn learns not to grab the wrong one when its owner comes around cursing and threatening.

It's an odd but understandable relationship between a planter and his tool. You develop a fondness for it over time. You get used to the feel of it, the weight and balance and grip of it in your hand. Some guys would rather hand over their wives.

On the steeper ground, the hoedag is a climbing tool, like a mountaineer's ice axe. It clears the way through heavy brush like a machete. You can lean on it like a cane to help straighten your sore back, and it is the weapon of choice when one is needed. It allows you to open up stumps and logs in search of the dark gold pitch that will start a fire in a cold downpour and to dig a quick fire trail if your break fire runs off up the hill.

The foreman hands out the big waxed cardboard boxes full of trees. The boxes are ripped open with a hoedag and you carry double handfuls of seedlings, wired up in bundles of fifty, over to the handiest puddle to wet down their roots. Dry roots will kill a tree before it can get into the ground, so the idea isn't purely a matter of adding extra weight to make the job harder — though that's the inevitable result.

Three hundred to four hundred trees get stuffed into the double bags, depending on their size and the length of the morning's run. If the nursery hasn't washed the roots properly before bundling and packing, the mud, added water, and trees can make for a load that is literally staggering.

No one puts on his bag until the boxes are burnt. It is an essential ritual and depriving a crew of its morning fire is, by ancient custom, held to be justifiable grounds for mutiny by crummy lawyers everywhere. Some argue that homicide in such a case would be ruled self-defense, but so far no one's ever tested it.

The waxed cardboard burns wonderfully bright and warm. A column of flame fifteen feet high lights up the road and everyone gathers around to take a little warmth and a lot of courage. Steam clouds rise from your rain gear as you rotate before the fire. It feels great and you need it, because once the flames turn to ashes you're going over the side.

"OK. Everybody get loaded and space-out," The Mouth calls out. You strap on your bag, tilt your tin hat, and grab your 'dag. You shuffle over to the edge of the road and line up eight feet from the man on each side.

## IN THE HOLE

The redoubtable Mighty Mouth plants in the lead spot, and the men behind him work in order from the faster to the slowest men. It is a shameful thing to plant slower than the guy behind you. If he's impatient, or out to score some points with the boss, he'll jump your line and you plant in his position, sink-ing lower in the Bull-of-the-woods standings. Slow planters get fired.

There are many tricks to appearing to be faster than you really are — stashing trees, widening your spacing, pushing the man behind you into the rougher parts while you widen or narrow your line to stay in the gravy — but all of these will get you in trouble one way or another, if not with the boss then, worse still, with the crew.

## CUMULATIVE IMPACT

It's best not to look at the clear-cut itself. You stay busy with whatever is immediately in front of you because, like all industrial processes, there is beauty in the details and ugliness in the larger view. Oil film on a rain puddle has an iridescent sheen that is lovely in a way that the junkyard it's part of is not.

Forests are beautiful on every level, whether seen from a distance or standing beneath the trees or studying a small patch of ground. Clear-cuts contain many wonderful things — jasper, petrified wood, sun-bleached bits of wood, bone and antler, wildflowers. But the sum of these finely wrought details adds up to a grim landscape, charred, eroded, and sterile.

Although tree planting is part of something called "reforestation," clear-cutting is never called "deforestation," at least not by its practitioners. The semantics of forestry doesn't allow that. The mountain slope is a "unit," the forest a "timber stand," logging is "harvest" and repeated logging "rotation."

On the work sheets foresters use is a pair of numbers that tracks the layers of canopy, the covering of branches and leaves that the trees have spread out above the soil. The top layer is called the overstory, beneath which is a second layer, the understory. A forest, for example, may have an overstory averaging a height of 180 feet and an understory of 75 feet. Clear-cuts are designated "Overstory: Zero."

In the language (and therefore the thinking) of industrial silviculture a clear-cut is a forest. The system does not recognize any depletion at all. The company is fond of talking about trees as a renewable resource, and the official line is that clear-cutting, followed by reforestation, results in a net gain.

"Old-growth forests are dying, unproductive forests — biological deserts full of diseased and decaying trees. By harvesting and replanting we turn them into vigorous, productive stands," the company forester will tell you. But ask if he's willing to trade company-owned old-growth forest for a clear-cut of the same acreage and the answer is always "No, of course not."

You listen and tell yourself that it's the company that treats the land shabbily. You see your work as a frenzied life-giving dance in the ashes of a plundered world. You think of the future and the green legacy you leave behind you. But you know that your work also makes the plunder seem rational and is, at its core, just another part of the destruction.

More than the physical exhaustion, this effort to not see the world tires you. It takes a lot of effort not to notice, not to care. When the world around you is painful and ugly, that pain and ugliness seeps into you, no matter how hard you try to keep it out. It builds up like a slowly accumulating poison. Sometimes the poison turns to venom and you strike out, as quick as any rattlesnake, but without the honest rattler's humane fair warning.

So you bitch and bicker with the guys on the crew, argue with the foreman, and snap at your wife and kids. You do violent work in a world where the evidence of violence is all around you. You see it in the scorched earth and the muddy streams. You feel it when you step out from the living forest into the barren clear-cut. It rings in your ears with the clink of steel on rock. It jars your arm with every stab of your hoedag.

## THE LONG MARCH

"War is hell," General Sherman said, because, unlike a Pentagon spokesman, he was in the midst of it and could not conceive of something so abstract as "collateral damage."

"Planting sucks," we say, because unlike the mill owner who signs our paychecks, we slog through the mud and bend our backs on mountain slopes instead of reading progress reports on reforestation units. Like infantry, we know weariness and hopelessness in the face of insanity.

"The millions of trees that the timber industry plants every year are enough to plant a strip four miles wide from here to New York," the foreman tells us.

Our hearts sink at the thought of that much clear-cutting but Madman Phil, the poet, sees a vision. "Forward, men!" he cries. "Shoulder to shoulder we march on New York. The American Tree Planter! Ever onward!"

Someone starts it, and then the whole crew is humming "The Battle Hymn of the Republic" while we work and Phil rants. In our minds, we cross the Cascades, the Snake River country, the Rockies, the Great Plains and onward, ever onward, a teeming, faceless coolie army led by Sasquatch and Mao Tse Tung, a barbarian horde leaving a swath of green behind us "from sea to shining sea."

"Oh, God!" Jimboy moans, "you guys are crazy."

# killed in the woods

The phone rings and you pick it up. You hear that a friend got killed in the woods, and those four words — killed in the woods — plunge down your spinal column like a cold steel blade.

They can't tell you right away how it happened, but getting killed in the woods is different from, say, dying in the woods. It doesn't happen to old men, and most likely the funeral will be closed-coffin. You recall others, friends or relatives, who got killed in the woods. *Tree split on him. Log shifted. Cable snapped. Trailer backed over him.*

John Keller was a logger, and he was a good one. Keller's early specialty was climbing and topping. With spiked boots and a climbing strap, his cutting tools dangling from his belt, he would climb the tallest and strongest tree in a stand. He would limb it on the way up, cut the top off and rig the tree as the spar pole for high-lead logging.

There are other dangerous jobs in the woods, but none where success or failure is quite so visible. Toppers tend to be exaggerated people. A tree-topper has to be strong and athletic and cool enough to apply a power saw at dizzying heights. He doesn't have to be a deep thinker, but he must react instantly to gusts of wind on a Cascade mountain slope. A good topper is brash and decisive, and it doesn't hurt if he likes to be the center of attention.

John Keller combined all of these traits. What was unusual about Keller was that his career as a topper started backwards. He began by falling.

Although Keller came from a family of loggers, he was not a logger himself at the time of his fall. Six years out of high school, in 1969, he was running a filling station in Estacada, often slipping off from the gas pumps to climb the spar pole at the Timber Festival site. Keller was what we called crazy, meaning he had not yet found himself. He was searching fast, in all the wrong places. John so loved the world that he tried to drink it all of one gulp — booze, pills, fast cars. The smart money said he wouldn't live twenty-seven years, much less the forty-seven he finally put in. He'd already survived rear-ending a school bus on his motorcycle.

And then the fall. On a dare, Keller entered the speed-climbing competition, novice division, at the 1969 Estacada Timber Festival. It was a sizzling day in July, and Keller addressed the spar pole in a beery haze, without having slept the night before.

Up the tree he went, boots spiking bark, his climbing strap skipping ahead of him around the tree. Seventy feet. Ninety feet up.

People who saw it — I didn't — will tell you he fell as if he were unconscious. But Keller insisted, later, he remembered falling. He remembered, at the top, thinking *This is a very bad time to black out.* He blacked out long enough for his spikes to lose their grip on bark. Both feet flipped out to one side, above his head, initiating the 100-foot drop to the base of the tree. He told me his life passed before him as if on a newsreel, just like it's supposed to, and he remembered bouncing at the bottom.

The bounce, more than the fall, is what they still talk about in Estacada. The bounce is what they remember. At the base of the tree was fresh sawdust over plywood, and Keller bounced six feet in the air or a third of the way back up the tree, depending on who you talk to.

On the ground, Keller wiggled a toe inside his boot. He shared the surprise and pleasure of those gathered over his body when they confirmed that he was — incredibly — alive. His being zonked, although it led to the climb in the first place, let him survive the fall.

The line between fool and hero in a small logging town is as fickle as anywhere else, but maybe a little easier to cross. Having already established, as he lay there, a shining place for himself in local folklore, Keller faced a dividing future. He could go on to become enormously foolish. Or, given his tools, he could be heroic. He could become a logger, that is.

And he did. Backwards — from the fall to the climb, from exhibition to work — Keller carved out a sober and lasting reputation for himself among Estacada woodsmen.

Twelve years passed between Keller's fall and the next time I saw him. It was 1981, and we both had work on our minds. I was trying to avoid work. I'd had my fill of a nine-to-five city job, and I figured maybe I could be a writer. Anybody could be a writer, I thought, if he knew a story. And the first true story that came to mind was John Keller and his reverse tree-topping career.

Keller had work on his mind because he was having trouble finding it.

Mechanical, telescoping spar poles of steel had all but silenced the call for tree-toppers, and 1981 was a terrible year, anyway, to find work in the woods. Now Keller was a cutter, a faller. And he had a bum back. He was using his down time to sell real estate. Real estate was all wrong for John. Keller was too agreeable and trusting to be a seller, and a white shirt and tie failed to disguise his true purpose, which lay in the woods. But you do what you have to do.

The surprise was that here was a guy I'd known earlier as a wild man, a screamer, a red Corvette speeding down a night road with no headlights. And here he was, someone else. When I caught up with him at his low, humid house on Springwater Road, he'd just finished shearing a sheep. In the front room, on a wall above the loom, was a glowing portrait of Jesus Christ. After John offered me a beer, he popped open a can of Pepsi for himself. He'd married Janis Salyers, a clear-eyed, no-nonsense, earth-mother beauty I would never have paired up with John. They had a kid. Keller could still laugh at himself — on the stereo was a raucous bit called "Loggin' and Lovin'" by the Cascade Mountain Boys — but the truth is he had left all foolishness behind.

If the woods picked up and he got his back straightened out, John allowed, he might get back to logging.

In a few years the woods did pick up. Keller went back to logging, gyppo logging. He would gather a crew and clear your back forty, say, or bid on a salvage job the big outfits passed up. Gyppo logging is a struggle. Just when he thought he was making ends meet, his second child was diagnosed with cystic fibrosis. Just when he thought he might be getting ahead, his business partner bailed out on him, leaving Keller with debts and back taxes he'd thought were paid.

Bad luck and good stories came to Keller like iron filings to a magnet. Two days after he bought a used Caterpillar D-4 and posted signs — CAT WORK — around town, he got a call from a lady whose cat was stuck in a tree. Keller scaled the tree and rescued the cat.

Through it all, John had a cheerfulness and serenity about him that could only come from a man who knew who he was. He could fill a room with that woodsy, easy-does-it grin of his, and make you glad to be there. In May, at our house in Portland, it was after a literary reading. I hadn't thought John would come, but he and Janis did. They brought the kids. He liked the porch better than inside, although he wasn't smoking. He held a 7-Up can with two hands between oaken axe-handle wrists. John could stand right there and still be distant, hearing new stories with a long and vaguely joyous face, his calm brown eyes — like what other people do is their business and he had a good seat for it. Men on the porch stood a little straighter, and women gulped.

When everybody left, Donna and I talked. Donna, too, has known John Keller since back when he was crazy, and she didn't know what it was. She said Janis and the kids had it, too. *What is it?* But the hour was late, and this was too hard for us. We forgot about it until the phone call.

The way he got killed, this September, was Keller was running his Cat on a steep grade, clearing road. A stand of vine maples bent easily under the uphill track. When he shifted direction, the physics of it favored the maples. The cocked trees sprang upward beneath the track, lifting that side of the Cat and throwing Keller to the ground.

The Cat rolled and crushed him.

Keller had been working some distance from his crew, and they didn't miss him for half an hour or so. When they did, and went to look, it was clear he got killed instantly.

We tend to surround ourselves with people who think the same way we do. Vote no on 9. Shut the nuclear plant down. Save the old-growth forests. In the crowd I run with, loggers are not heroes. They are brute killers of trees. So the short life of John Keller goes beyond a hard pull on the heartstrings. It loosens your headstrings. The death of a distant friend makes you wonder, and what it makes you wonder about is the nature of work.

The choice for me, early, was college or work. It never occurred to me, leaving Estacada for college, that I would never be back, that I would come to view work as something that happens on the other side of a great chasm. Most people I know lift nothing heavier than the phone book and wield tools no more dangerous than a corkscrew. Shame, more than anything, might account for the draw of people who work on people who don't, for the yuppification of country music, for the high place of boots and denim in fashion. Or maybe you have to be an exile from that working culture to even make the connection, to know in your bones that people who work are the real people.

"John was a logger," says Norman Christensen, a logger. "His pants were stagged off at a good length, a bit ragged and well-worn. If you got close you could smell the sawdust, the work. His rigging truck looked just like him — run hard and put away wet. In summer he ate dust. In the fall he was wet from morning 'til night. In the dead of winter he was cold to the bone and had to work fast and hard to keep warm."

"You couldn't find a better man to work with," says Mike Perry, a logger. "Things break down. You get fuck-ups. John could shrug it off. 'That's logging,' he would say. Keller's dad, too, got killed in the woods.

"But still, John loved it," Christensen says. "Logging gets in your body and you can't get it out. At first light, when the sun comes up behind Mount Hood and the birds start chirping and the air is cool, you can feel it go down in your lungs. The smell of the woods as it's being logged. The men you work with who feel the same way you do."

It makes you wonder, too, about a peculiar wholeness that comes to those who deal on a life-and-death basis with nature. This is not fly-casting. Not canoeing. This is not politically correct. Logging is a way of life that has built what we have of myth — life is hard in the West — and birthed the angst we know as culture. Maybe it's the very contact with woods, this terrible intimacy with trees, that gave John's life purpose and order. We can question the purpose, but not the order. I think of Barry Lopez, in an entirely different context, writing about how an enduring relationship with landscape is essential to a balanced state of mental health.

"He loved those kids," says Perry. "If it was Saturday, he took them along. John would take his little ones out to the woods with him. They must have got up at three o'clock. *You kids stay in the truck.*"

"John knew what he had," Christensen says, "and it was enough. It was a lot. It was his family and his work. When he shook your hand, you knew you had a man on the other end."

# ADRIAN RAESIDE

# correspondence and conversations concerning the former mrs. kosiki

Poverty is the great reality. That is why the artist seeks it.
— *Anais Nin*

388-49-300; Food stamps are authorized for the children *only*. You fail to meet the criteria for the food stamp program. Be sure to report the amount of child support you will be receiving when your decree is final.
— *D. Bush, Financial Service Specialist*

I will send you your contributor's copy as soon as I get the first run back from the printer.
— *Brian Christopher Hamilton, Editor,* Rain City Review

"I want Nike Airs for school this year."
— *John*

We are in the process of reviewing your AMCO homeowner's policy. We feel a responsibility to make you aware of our concern regarding your policy. We noted that your bikes were stolen from your detached storage shed on September 7. AMCO's preferred rates are based on the expectancy of few losses. We will be sending a representative to your home to assess it and verify its condition. We are sure you understand the necessity to insure appropriately so that you obtain the full value of your policy in the event of a loss.
— *William Sundstrom, Underwriting Department, AMCO Mutual Insurance Company*

"Want a latte?"
— *Kate*

**104** There is remaining an outstanding dental bill which Mr. Allan Kosiki indicates he anticipates paying at such time as this matter is finalized. He plans on making $40.00 per month payments on that obligation.
— *Frank Jefferies, Attorney*

REMINDER  NOTICE
For some reason your account is now on the "Delinquent List."
— *Molli, The Office of Adam Mills, DDS*

We regret that we are unable
to use the enclosed material.
Thanks for giving us the
opportunity to consider it.
— *The Editors*, The New Yorker

"I'm not standing in line with you if you're going to pay for that with food stamps."
— *Jessica*

In your paperwork you sent a worksheet that imputed income to Mrs. Kosiki of about $1,400.00 per month. As you know, Mrs. Kosiki is a writer...
— *R. Samuel Murphy, Attorney*

We have received the property inspection report which indicates that your dwelling is well maintained. The inspector noted that your roof has become worn and will need to be replaced soon. We are advising you of this matter to help protect you from any loss which may occur from this situation. When you have had your roof replaced, send a photograph or copy of a receipt. Until then, we will not be ABLE TO cover any losses that result from damage to the roof.
— *William Sundstrom, Underwriting Department, AMCO Mutual Insurance Company*

"I'll just put this meat in the freezer."
— *Dad*

Your contributor copies should be arriving in about two months.
—*Christian Reiten, Editor, Oregon East*

You fail to meet the criteria for medical assistance. However, your children qualify.
— *Alice Bates, Caseworker*

"Your auto rates are increasing by $100 because you no longer qualify for the multi-car discount, not, as you assert, because you are no longer married.

"I have referred your question about the homeowner policy to that department."
— *Policy Agent, AMCO*

Allan Kosiki called on Monday. He believes he only owes $75.00 on the Visa bill based on the balance owing at the time of separation.
— *Frank Jefferies, Attorney*

"Where did you get this peanut butter? It's all stiff and won't spread."
— *John*

This is to inform you that we have not yet received the payment on your account. You are now more than 15 days past due.
— *Collection Department, Bank of New York (Delaware), Visa accounts*

"I'm afraid I don't understand what Jessica finds embarrassing about asking for her free lunch ticket when she's in line with the gifted students. Perhaps she should be in my self-esteem group on Wednesdays."
— *Muffy Morris, Guidance Counselor*

"I'll get the parking."
— *Kate*

"When I called for confirmation on your Visa card, they said your account had been canceled. Is there some other way you'd like to pay for these printer ribbons?"
— *Operator, Micro Resources*

"I am sorry, but I cannot verify that you applied for this account in your own name. According to our records, this was a joint account. Therefore, your husband can cancel it."
— *Customer service, Bank of New York (Delaware), Visa Accounts*

"This cough syrup is not covered by medical coupons."
— *Orville Hanson, Southside Drug*

"This is the last time I can fix the dishwasher. If it breaks again, you'll have to get a new one."

| Labor — repair dishwasher | $37.50 |
| --- | --- |
| TOTAL | $37.50 |

—*Jim, Golden Appliance Repair*

"Want a latté?"
— *Kate*

This is a clever idea for a parody, but it doesn't seem quite right for our pages, alas. Sorry, and thanks for letting us look.
— *The Editors*, The New Yorker

"There are no more slots available for energy assistance. If you receive a shut-off notice, we may be able to help."
— *Receptionist, Community Action and Assistance*

"You need any zucchini?"
— *Arnie, Neighbor*

We pay in contributor copies.
— *Editor*

"You're driving on expired plates."
— *Officer Mary Bates*

"I can give you $69.00 for the proof sets."
— *Darrell Lindemann, The Mint Coin Shop*

"Keep the shovel and garden hose, they were just cluttering up the garage anyway."
— *Arnie, Neighbor*

"Seldane is no longer covered by medical coupons."
— *Orville Hanson, Southside Drug*

"Get a job."
— *Allan*

"Just bring the car over on Sunday and we'll see what's wrong with it. It doesn't sound too serious."
— *Dan*

You do not qualify for Telephone Assistance because you do not receive food stamps. Someone in the household over 18 years of age must be receiving food stamps.
— *Pacific Northwest Bell*

"It needs a clutch, for sure."
— *Dan*

"This inhaler is not covered by medical coupons."
— *Orville Hanson, Southside Drug*

Sorry. Again.
— *David Waggoner, Editor,* Poetry Northwest

"I clocked you at thirty-five in a twenty-five zone. That's a $75 fine in College Place. Court is on Tuesday."
— *Officer Robert S. Trapp*

"You leave the tip. I'll get the check."
— *Kate*

"I *may* be able to back your data onto a new hard drive."
— *Aaron, New Age Technical*

Sorry we couldn't use this material, it came close. Please submit again in December for our February issue.
— *Dennis Held, Editor,* CutBank

| | |
|---|---|
| Hard drive (60 meg.) | $220.00 |
| Installation | 75.00 |
| TOTAL | $300.00 |

— *Aaron, New Age Technical*

I wish I could send more.
— *Grandma*

"Call a plumber. We're not married any more."
— *Allan*

| | |
|---|---|
| Snake drain, replace pipe in basement | $125.00 |
| Parts | 16.50 |
| TOTAL | $141.50 |

— *Marv, Skip Barlow's Plumbing*

"I'm collecting for the American Heart Association."
— *Neighbor*

"I'm collecting canned goods for the needy."
— *Boy Scout*

"Here's a turkey. Merry Christmas from Church."
— *Tony Navarre*

I enjoyed your reading at the Poetry Party. You must be published in many journals and literary magazines. Which ones? Your work is of an unusually high order for a regional poet and I hope your editors are telling you the same. Have a happy new year.
— *Jon Hui, A Fan in Salem*

"$36 cash or $42 trade."
— *Powell's Ponytail*

"Want a latte?"
— *Kate*

KYLE WALKER

# the price
# of free speech
## AN INTERVIEW WITH SANDY NELSON

She calls herself a prisoner of war — management's prisoner in a war over the rights of journalists to be political activists on their own time.

Tacoma journalist Sandy Nelson was an award-winning education reporter at the Morning News Tribune, *Washington's third-largest daily newspaper. In her off hours, she was an organizer for Radical Women, a socialist-feminist organization founded in the Northwest in 1967. Active for years in abortion-clinic defense and the defense of Native American treaty rights, in the fall of 1990 Nelson was involved in a grass-roots initiative campaign to reinstate anti-discrimination protections for lesbians and gay men in Tacoma.*

*In September 1990, MNT management transferred Nelson from writing to a swing shift copyediting job, saying her political activism compromised the newspaper's "appearance of objectivity" even though Nelson never wrote about the campaign. When the initiative failed in November, upholding the legality of anti-gay discrimination in Tacoma, Nelson was told she would stay on the copy desk until she ceased all off-duty political activities.*

*The American Civil Liberties Union of Washington recently agreed to represent Nelson in her ongoing fight for reinstatement to reporting. The ACLU is prepared to sue for violation of Nelson's constitutional rights in what would be an unprecedented case for the free-speech rights of journalists.*

**Kyle Walker**: What is "objectivity" in reporting?

**Sandy Nelson**: Reporters can, and do, exercise basic democratic rights as citizens and still write fair and balanced news. In eleven years as a reporter at two newspapers, I never was reprimanded for biased writing, and all that time I have been an outspoken advocate of women's rights, civil rights, and unionism. I feel reporters, like other workers, should be judged on the basis of what we produce, not how we feel or what we do off the job. Management's objectivity argument is a ruse, a smoke screen behind which they punish workers who become involved in union organizing or community organizing outside the mainstream. It's an excuse to discriminate against classes of people, such as women, gay men and lesbians, people of color, whose political involvement is a matter of survival on and off the job, not a hobby. It's an excuse to weed out radicals, just as radicals were the first to be purged from the media and communications industries during the McCarthy era. Media managers increasingly are using ethical pretexts to muddy the waters as they impose round-the-clock control of journalists' lives.

KW: Doesn't the newspaper sponsor community events, and isn't the publisher encouraged to be involved in the community?

SN: Yes on both counts. Which underscores the double standard of the so-called "objectivity" standard. The publisher and top management are free to be involved in influential community groups and policymaking boards while reporters are expected to keep our thoughts to ourselves and not get involved in our communities — unless it's with the Boy Scouts, our churches, or Little League. But all of these groups are political at one time or another. *News Tribune* management believes it has the right to decide what politics we are allowed to be involved in, and at what level.

KW: Isn't there such a thing as a conflict of interest? Do you believe you can be involved in the stories you write about?

SN: My definition of a conflict of interest is much narrower than management's. Theirs is so broad it goes beyond the realm of reality into fantasy, prohibiting conflicts and involvements that have the potential to appear to be conflicts. I endorse a more material, tangible definition. To me, a conflict of interest or appearance of conflict exists only when a journalist stands to gain personally or financially from a story she writes or edits. It's that simple.

As for whether reporters should write stories about issues they're involved in: yes. Personally, I believe a reporter with firsthand knowledge about the issue he or she is reporting is better equipped to write an informative story and even a balanced one. The line I always walked in the mainstream media is that I informed management whenever an assignment overlapped into my off-hour activities; in more than twelve years as a reporter I can count on one hand the times that happened. Occasionally, management directed me to go ahead and write the story, and sometimes we informed the readers by way of an editor's note at the beginning. It is not so complicated to do. The newspapers are full of first-person accounts and editors' notes. Studies have shown that readers care less about what journalist do on their own time than they do about fair and balanced reporting. Readers understand that all journalists have biases; they ask simply that their biases not color their presentations of facts and information.

KW: How long have such standards been in place at the *Morning News Tribune* and in the newspaper industry?

SN: The *Morning News Tribune* ethics code is still only in draft form, though a hand-picked committee began writing it in 1986, after the company was sold to McClatchy, Inc. and our union contracts were abrogated. The first draft came under fire by newsroom employees, who demanded it become part of negotiations for a new contract with the Pacific Northwest Newspaper Guild, Local 82. It contained broad prohibitions against off-duty political activities and even voting rights. Nothing happened with the code until after my transfer (on the basis of controversial "standards" in the unratified code) and after the Guild was decertified in August 1991. At that time, management picked another ethics committee to redraft the code. My co-workers, mindful of what had happened to me, became more involved in the process, and what emerged — still in draft form — is much less intrusive than the original. It's still not acceptable to me, but at least it requires management to seek the least-intrusive remedy to conflicts and recognizes that employees have the right to be involved in the initiative and referendum process, as I was at the time of my transfer.

These "standards," by no means universal, are also recent developments in the industry. Most ethics codes have been adopted only in the past twenty years as the industry struggles to develop standards of professionalism. Some of the ethical standards are legitimate where they prohibit freebies, bribes, and other acts of corruption. But those that attempt to control off-hours activities are illegitimate because they function to command obedience and servitude among people whose obedience should be only to truthful and aggressive reporting.

KW: How has the Guild intervened in your fight?

SN: The Guild filed a complaint with the National Labor Relations Board right after my transfer, arguing that the *Morning News Tribune* had unilaterally imposed an unratified ethics code. The Guild also argued that the code went too far in its prohibition of off-duty activities, that it wasn't narrowly tailored to protect only the legitimate business interests of the paper. The NLRB refused to hear the case even though it was appealed twice to the board's national office in Washington, D.C. But the Guild has remained steadfast, even after the local was decertified in a management union-busting campaign in 1991. The International Executive Board of the Newspaper Guild in October 1992 passed a resolution in support of my case, joining the Seattle Guild local and many other unions as endorsers. Emmett Murray, president of the Seattle local, remains one of my greatest supporters, partly because he experienced similar censorship at the *Seattle Times*.

KW: How is your case similar to other cases where employers claim the right to control the off-duty activities of workers?

SN: Employers increasingly are testing their ability to control not just the hours an employee spends at work but also the time he or she spends off the job. Employers are forcing the people who work for them — as a condition of employment — to submit to lie detector tests, drug tests, cholesterol tests, and tests that determine if a worker is smoking at home. Employers are a greater threat to civil liberties these days than the government is, partly because they get away with things government couldn't get away with. The media industry is increasingly striking out against reporters who exercise their most basic political rights off the job — the right to speak freely, the right to protest, the right to assemble and associate freely — the very rights media owners claim to revere. Linda Greenhouse of the *New York Times* was reprimanded for participating in the 1989 March on Washington for Women's Lives. Former United Press International reporter Julie Brienza was fired from her job more than two years ago for "freelancing" after she exposed a right-wing talk-show host in an article for a lesbian and gay publication in Washington, D.C. Vicky Hendley was fired from a newspaper in a small Florida town in the late 1980s after she sent coat hangers to her legislators in protest of anti-abortion laws. The list goes on, and it's growing faster as times get harder and the economy deteriorates.

KW: Doesn't the constitution protect workers from such actions by management?

SN: The U.S. Constitution prohibits government from abridging First Amendment rights, but it doesn't explicitly prohibit private employers from doing the same thing. I see no difference between government and the business class it serves, and I hope my case can bridge that gap and help advance arguments for protection from employment discrimination on the basis of political ideology. Many states and cities, including Seattle, have such laws. Luckily, the Washington state constitution has strong free-speech provisions that have been upheld against private entities. We will rely on these protections, among other things.

KW: How do readers respond to your fight?

SN: Thousands of *Morning News Tribune* readers and thousands of other people from across the country — and in other countries — have signed petitions demanding the *Morning News Tribune* reinstate me to reporting. Many have written letters to *Morning News Tribune* managers and attempted to meet with the publisher to argue for my reinstatement. Newspaper readers realize their stake in having reporters who understand the issues that impact their lives and their communities. Some of them even consider involved reporters better reporters.

KW: How have lesbian and gay activists responded to your plight?

SN: I have been gratified by the support from rank-and-file gay activists and the mass gay movement. *Seattle Gay News* broke the story of my transfer when most newspapers wouldn't touch it. I spoke at the Seattle Gay and Lesbian Pride March in 1991 and at the OutWrite Conference in Boston in 1992. Those who understand that my case is a gay-rights issue have been immediately supportive. But gay and lesbian activists whose first concern is appearing respectable to the heterosexual mainstream have been cooler and more distant. I'm sure it's because I'm a socialist.

KW: How does it feel to be working for an employer you're preparing to sue? How are you treated by managers and co-workers?

SN: Every day that I go to work, I feel like I'm going to war. Management continues a guerrilla war against me by giving me substandard evaluations after refusing training; my most recent evaluation denied me a raise for the second year in a row. They hope to wear me down and drive me out. What makes it worthwhile are my co-workers. Regardless of their own practices off the job, the majority of them are watching my case with a great deal of interest. Many are openly supportive. They realize they have a stake in the outcome.

These are hard times to be a radical, to oppose capitalism. These are times that test people's values and principles. I consider my personal and professional crisis a tremendous opportunity to expose the myth of objectivity, to speak out against bosses who trample on the civil liberties of workers and to make common cause with readers for a more responsive and responsible media. A free press requires free reporters — now more than ever.

# occupational hazards

Working graveyard shift at a 7–11
in Seattle, making minimum
everything, when I got robbed

by a guy with a pistol. Now
I was thinking as it happened
thinking the gun ain't loaded

everything is under control
this guy don't want to hurt me
he understands I ain't got much

more than he does. I got
an old car, high rent, even
the same dark skin as his

and my best shirt is the one
I have to wear to work
with 7–11 stitched on my chest.

But the robber takes me back
into the cooler, makes me
kneel on the cold floor

with my hands on my head/ my back turned to him/ and I wet
my pants when he puts the pistol/ up against my skull/ I keep
thinking/ I'm going to die/ between the broken eggs/ and the
expired milk/ and I keep thinking/ I'll make a move/ on the
robber/ and tear the gun from him/ and I keep thinking/ I'd
rather die fighting/ and I'd rather die brave and crazy

but the robber laughs, runs
out of the store, out
of the rest of my life

# occupational hazards

and leaves me to the police
and their sketch artist.
It takes hours to describe

the robber, detail by detail
the color of his hair, eyes, skin
his height, weight, age

all approximated, estimated.
After all that work
the sketch artist asks

if I've remembered everything
perfectly, if I'm sure
I've described the robber

exactly as he looked, exactly
as he lived and breathed
and I tell the sketch artist

*Yes, I could never forget*
and then he shows me his sketch
shows me my memory, my vision

and the face on the page
is the same face I always see
when I look in my mirror

in those last seconds
before I walk out the door
and leave home for work.

# ADRIAN RAESIDE

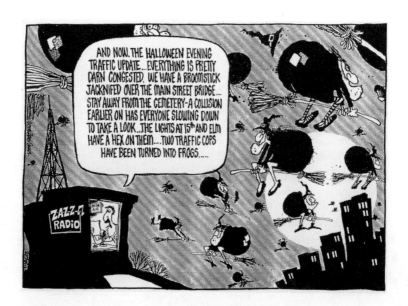

JOAN SHOGAN

# the redemption
# of nick carriere

I think about Nick Carriere almost every night now when I can't sleep. First I think about my husband and how I left him and found another man and then left him. I go over the lying I've done to get money. Lie is too strong a word, I tell myself. I mean exaggerating the truth, fudging and softening and blurring it on government forms and applications for jobs and loans. Then I switch to thinking about Nick. The way he told it, he's walking in the Garden of Eden right here on earth now, after years in the wilderness, but his happy ending doesn't comfort me the way I always think it will.

The ferry was getting out into Milbanke Sound, and Nick and Tommy Jack and I were the only ones left in the bar. This was last March, after herring.

"It was a dark and stormy night," Nick said solemnly, then he laughed and pulled back the heavy curtain so we could look out into the black and hear the crash of the sea. Tommy grinned. I used to know his father years ago in Alert Bay, and they look alike. Nick was a stranger to me, but he seemed peaceful enough. His eyes were light gray, like mine.

We were all quiet for a while, holding on to our glasses and watching the floor tilt back and forth. "You were fishing at Kitkatla?" I asked. Tommy nodded, and he and Nick talked about the boats that had been there and the pools they were in and how much their own shares might be. Maybe I looked as if I were listening, but I wasn't. I was thinking about the last time I had crossed Milbanke Sound, getting a free ride south along with the chum salmon on a pig of a steel packer with a skipper to match. I walked off in Namu and demanded a different boat. I had been able to afford a high horse when I was still married to a good fisherman. I hitched my chair into the circle of light around the table and wondered if any other boats were traveling in the heaving darkness outside the curtained window.

Nick and Tommy were silent again. After a bit, I said, "Prices not bad, eh?" and Tommy told me the gillnet and seine prices for a ton of herring. I tried to look calm, as if I were expecting to help spend someone's crew share check, same as usual. Nick looked past Tommy and me onto the polished square of the empty dance floor.

"I had to fish for the Royal Bank once," he said. Tommy and I waited. I can't say if I knew it would be a funny story or a sad one, though Nick's mouth was already set in a hard line. I don't think even Nick knew, at the start, that he was going to line up his last thirty years and mark them off with stories like signposts on the road to where he lives now.

"Fishing for the Royal Bank," Nick repeated. "This was maybe thirty years ago, the branch at Main and Hastings. Fishermen are always saying they're fishing for the bank, eh. Paying off their boat loans. But this bank was actually giving the orders. They had a hold on Eddie and John Johansen for the *Katherine A.* and they wouldn't take the boat back — no market — and they wouldn't let go. It was, 'Take the boat out again. Find fish. Make money.'" Maybe Tommy was listening because there was nothing else to listen to. He might not have had that much experience with banks. But I was paying close attention. I like a good bank story.

Nick went on. "This was in November. Eddie and John — Johnny's dead now — they'd gone broke buying salmon in the Charlottes, and I'd been on the boat with them since May. I'd never have got any of my share if I quit them then. No other jobs around anyway. Only thing we had gear for that was around that time of year was dogfish." Nick sighed. Tommy and I looked sympathetic. A story with dogfish and the Royal Bank and November in it was not going to end well.

Nick passed lightly over six weeks' long-lining in the Straits. Wind. Rain. Cold. More potatoes than anything else to eat. Some dogfish. Eight cents a pound, dressed. The *Katherine A.* didn't make grub and fuel. "Two days before Christmas we dumped the last load at Campbell Avenue. Walked up to the bank. They had a young fellow in there, real snotty, with a nice suit."

Nick's voice stayed quiet, but he spat out his words like birdshot. "'We need a drag,' Eddie says to this young banker. 'A drag,' the banker says back. 'What's a drag?'" Nick stopped for a moment so we could take this in. I thought about it. The Royal Bank had apparently thought that being a fishing company meant sending its boat out to work but having nothing to do with the men who had to kneel on her deck and fillet dogfish in the rain.

"Finally," said Nick, "the little banker caught on. 'You can have twenty-five dollars,' he said. Eddie and John didn't say nothing, just stared at the floor. Too beat down, I guess. But I grabbed the little prick and lifted him off his feet. 'That's not enough for a hooker and a steak,' I yelled, 'and how are we supposed to get home for Christmas?'"

Tommy chuckled softly and Nick smiled, but his mouth returned right away to its tight line. I wondered what was coming next. I figured the big money on this year's herring had put Nick in mind of harder times, and he didn't look, right then, as if he were finished remembering them.

Tommy went up to the bar to get us more drinks, and I watched him coming back, walking easily, even with the floor slanting and dropping under him, and lifting the three glasses a little at the bottom of the roll so they wouldn't spill when the ship rose again. He sat down, and Nick said, "My son was born not too long after." The baby was fine at first, Nick told us, then something went wrong. He took a year to die. This was before the medical plan, so the bills were high.

Nick got the money robbing banks. The Kingsway and Knight branch of the Bank of Montreal and the one on Columbia Street in New Westminster; the Bank of Nova Scotia at Main and Second; the Toronto Dominion out in Abbotsford and the Bank of Commerce in Ladner, plus four or five more. "No Royal Banks," Nick said. "Coincidence. Not in the right place at the right time." Doing banks was not that tough, Nick assured us.

"Did you get caught?" I asked. Nick laughed.

"Do enough banks and for sure you'll get caught," he answered. Tommy looked thoughtful, and I tried to look as though I knew that all along. As for Nick, remembering prison didn't seem to bother him. Maybe he looked on jail as a natural consequence of bank robbing, just something to be postponed as long as possible.

The ferry heeled hard, and Tommy reached out to save the ashtray. I got up and went to the bar to get a coffee. Nick and Tommy didn't want anything. When I got back to the table, they were both laughing. I didn't ask why.

Nick was in jail a long time. When he got out, he hooked up with a friend who had a log salvage license. "You know how they work?" Nick asked me. "Used to work, anyway. A log salvage license and a chain saw and you're in business. A license to steal. We were putting together a boom, see. Courtesy of Mac, and Blo, and Rayonier. Get thirty-five, maybe forty thousand for it. We just needed someone to back us for the tug and the fuel. So I got five thousand from a guy I knew in Vancouver. Guaranteed him it would triple in a month."

Six weeks later the boom lay in a bay south of Powell River and Nick and his partner and the man from Vancouver were sitting on the bed in a room in the Austin Hotel on Granville Street. "Had the money," Nick said. "No problem. Thirty-seven thousand. Fifteen for the guy who backed us. Eleven each for my partner and me. I'm just counting out the fifteen when the door flies open. In comes a guy carrying a chunk. Points it at the guy who backed us. Says, 'He owes me.' Who's going to argue? I made a move to hand over the stack, twelve thousand and some. 'No,' says the guy with the gun. 'Take him over by the window.' So we do. Guy says, 'He goes out and you two get your share. If I have to do it, you get nothing.'"

Nick looked into my eyes for the first time. "What would you do?" he said to me. I stared back at him. I knew, even then, that he wanted me to say there was common ground between us. He knew what I would have done. I'm certain he knew. The backer was gone whatever Nick, or I, would have decided to do. I didn't answer and he didn't ask again.

In a low voice Nick said that he had hit the backer very hard on the side of the neck, then he and his partner opened the window on the fourth floor of the Austin Hotel and shoved him out.

Nick got up and went to the washroom and was gone for a long time. Tommy drew his chair closer to mine and searched his shirt pocket. He took out a handful of wooden matches and arranged them on the table to make fish shapes with squared-off fins. "There," he murmured. "Sockeye swimming north. See if you can move four matches and make them swim south." I stared at the matchstick fish for a long time before I reached out to move one match. My hand shook. "That's right," Tommy said encouragingly, "that's a start." Then he said, very quietly, "Nicky's a good man on the boat. He's all right. Don't say anything too hard to him. " I nodded my head.

Nick sat down with us again. It was after midnight by then, and the swell had gone down. We were almost across the Sound. Nick was watching me and I sat very still. He spoke slowly. "I was in Lillooet a while afterwards. Never been there before or since. I was helping my uncle move some stuff. We went into the Legion." My back was beginning to ache from being held so stiffly. "There was a woman in the Legion," Nick said. "Japanese. Shy. Always lived in Lillooet, never been in the Legion before in her life."

Nick pulled back the blackout curtain and held it so I could see over his shoulder. Outside was as black as ever, but the sound of the waves had fallen. When he turned back from the window, his face looked smoother, younger. "I thought it was all over when I got back to Vancouver, and the cops picked me up for some court show I missed. My uncle told her about it. She sent down the bail money."

Tommy seemed relaxed, not surprised. I suppose I wasn't that startled, either. From the start of the Lillooet story, Nick had looked happier, his mouth in a gentle curve. Nick and the Japanese woman live in Nanoose, in a house hidden off the road. Nick has worked on the same seine boat for herring and salmon more than ten years now, and he makes good money. He tells the fishing company to send his checks straight home. Nick said the woman has been cautious and clever with the money. They own another place as well as their own house and are quite secure, the two of them.

When I can't sleep, I prop all four pillows behind my head so I'm half sitting up in the dark. After I'm done remembering my husband and the other man and lies about money, I start on Nick Carriere's stories, certain that I'll be able to rest if I can come to understand why Nick got lucky or received the grace of God or whatever it was that provided the Japanese woman. She saved him, after all. Redeemed him.

I get up and fill the kettle for tea on particularly long nights. While I wait for the water to boil, I stand by the bookcase in the hall, running my fingers along the top row of books, looking, perhaps, as if I might choose any one of them. Then I pull out the dictionary and check once more. "Redeem: To recover by expenditure of effort or buy back one's rights, position, honor, or pledged goods. To purchase the freedom of another or oneself. Of God or Christ: To deliver from sin or damnation. To make amends for, counterbalance, or compensate." The dictionary says nothing of how to earn redemption.

When I drink my tea and finish with the night on the ferry last March, when I have remembered everything about Milbanke Sound and Nick's face and Tommy's matchstick fish, it is that unearned, accidental quality about Nick's happiness that denies me the comfort of believing it could happen to me. Nick did nothing to deserve the Japanese woman. He told the truth. I give him that.

I smooth the sheets and lie down again and pretend the bed is rocking on a gentle swell. I open my eyes to see if the sky is lighter yet and wonder if I would still be married if I'd known how this would be. I listen for the sound of the waves on my imagined sea, but most nights I can hear only the hard grinding of the stones on the bottom.

I was in Lillooet last May. I stopped at the Legion, but there was nothing there for me, and I drove through to the coast that same night.

TOM WAYMAN

# they made my city into two cities

## VANCOUVER

They made my city into two cities
I was watching but they did it anyway
One city with the sea breeze pouring up
through the clean streets
shadowed by enormous chestnut and cedar trees
under which are expensive boutiques and restaurants
houses costing so much you feel unworthy just looking at them
And down at the harbor, marinas full of boats priced
almost as high as the houses
with pennants flying gaily from masts
and from the balconies of taverns, import shops
and even food markets
catering exclusively to the rich
And to the east
is the other city
sidewalks cracked and patched
the trees spindly, discount merchandise for sale
and no ocean
except an industrial waterfront
vigilantly protected by the Ports police:
grain elevators, fish canneries, warehouses
with fences and railroad yards to keep you
as distant as possible from what might have been beaches
The avenues are stifling, if it isn't raining
the bars jammed and smoky
and, outside, the buses drag us from place to place
looking for work, like defective goods
being offered as joblots to various junk dealers

Even the mountains to the north, that on the west side
sparkle beautifully
here look vaguely menacing, like a health care premium
        increase
or a cut in welfare
The massive peaks seem like duties or procedures
we're going to have to fulfil
to stay out of jail

*Wait just a minute,* I can hear you saying
*Weren't there always two cities?*
And who are the "they" you're blaming
again for the world's troubles?

Yes, there were always two cities: the wealthy and the poor
But I grew up here, and don't remember
the gap so large
I don't recall businesses like the take-out Italian
        restaurant
that announced they would not deliver east of Main
or the monthly magazine issued by the largest newspaper
distributed only to the western half of my city
(You should have read the paper's consumer columnist
justifying this — how we'd all benefit
since the increased revenues would result in an improved daily
        product
even for east enders, blah blah blah)
There was certainly a ritzy neighborhood or two
but I don't remember the quarantining of so many districts
to eliminate anyone not rolling in money
as inflated house prices result
in only a tiny percentage of human beings
being able to live there
I don't remember this situation
encouraging real estate profiteers
to demolish what cheaper dwellings survive in every
        neighborhood
and to replace them with staggeringly expensive apartments and
        homes
I know a swath was never cut through the east side
to build a little toy elevated train

to deliver we slaves to our downtown jobs faster
(since house costs have forced us to live further and further
           from work)

Somebody kept insisting how wonderful this elevated system
was going to be, though they had to trash the bus service
to get enough of us to ride on it
to justify its existence
and a special tax had to be added onto both gasoline
and our electricity bill
to help subsidize such a marvel
Best of all were the cries of outrage
that went up from the west side
when it was proposed the little train should cut through
*their* neighborhoods
to connect with a suburb to the south into which
more of us had been pushed
"Not on your life!" the howl went up.
"Who do you think we are? *Who*
*do you think we are?*"

And that question brings us to your other point:
who *are* the "they"
that tore my city into two
(and who, as far as I can tell,
would be happy if they could eradicate the poorer half
           entirely
leaving this place restricted to the well-heeled)?
This is a question that's bothered me most of my life:
who decided that those who own an enterprise
should get more money than the rest of us who work at it each
           day?
I'm not talking about the wage structure, understand
I know each of us can construct dozens of excuses
why we should be paid more than the women or men working
           alongside us
No problem there (though this is what helps keep
the majority of us earning a lot less than we could be)
I'm talking about *decisions*: who, and how was it, determined
my city should be two cities?

Some people blame it on offshore money:

Japanese yen with nowhere else to be spent
Hong Kong dollars that have to be extracted from the colony
before the Chinese government at last reclaims
what belongs to its people
On the east side, graffiti expresses this viewpoint
with the area's usual delicate regard for personal feelings:
"Chinks hired? You're fired!"
the walls say. On the west side, the matter
is handled a little differently
such as when the federal government gave the Bank of Hong Kong
five million dollars "to financially assist"
their purchase of the Bank of B.C.
Such solidarity among the wealthy
— sharing around the trough of public money
for their own profit — regardless of skin color
or national origin
maybe expresses a healthier outlook, however,
than ours
For aren't we all immigrants
except for the tribes we hurt so viciously?
How can we draw a line and say:
"Now that I'm here, everybody else who arrives
is an alien life form"?
In any case, for every overseas arrival who buys in
somebody local must have sold out
Are the latter folks, then, the elusive "they"
I want to blame?
I observe how men and women from the other city
keep showing up where we live
to try to talk land prices higher and higher
and to convince people to open upscale catering enterprises
only a few blocks from the Food Bank lines
Probably the next step will be to operate charter bus tours
to bring tourists to watch our frenzies on Cheque Day
which some west siders like to regard as
a sort of Carnival
and which I'm sure the provincial Ministry of Tourism
would like to see expanded
into parades, floats, street dances
a monthly Mardi Gras

instead of shouting and glass breaking in the street
tires screeching, people staggering blankly around
or being sick on the sidewalk
falling down, or lurching past bleeding
from a skinned forehead and cut knuckles
or with eyes blackened and a broken nose
being hauled into wagons by the cops
or directed by social workers to an already-full women's
    shelter

Now if you think we're not getting too far
in determining who so transformed my city
maybe I can rephrase the issue:

why should there be
some men and women with too much money
and others with not enough?
Why isn't wealth, in a rich province
shared more equally? Can't we figure out
how to redistribute what we all help earn
or is it that we don't want to?
Anyway, why should the gulf between the cities
get wider and wider? Where do we go
if we can't afford to live in our neighborhood any longer?
Why should we have to leave?

Gee, this is like a quiz
Twenty-five points for each right answer!
And if nobody can come up with the correct response
I'll finish with a few additional questions:

what's wrong with there being one city of the very well off
and one of the increasingly poor?
Who has the power to change it?
Who *should* have the power to change it?
How do we stop
what's happening to us?

KEVIN BEZNER

# right work
## AN INTERVIEW WITH GARY SNYDER

Gary Snyder was born in San Francisco in 1930. He grew up in Oregon, was a student at Portland's Lincoln High, and in 1951 graduated from Reed College. Snyder then studied anthropology in graduate school; worked as a member of a Yosemite trail crew in the fifties; associated with Kerouac, Ginsberg, and others as part of the San Francisco Renaissance of the fifties; studied Zen Buddhism in Japan; and traveled in India, the Japan Sea, and in California from 1956 to 1968. During these years, Snyder held a wide variety of jobs. In addition to working on a trail crew, he was a forest-fire lookout, a ship's hand, and a logger. Throughout the years, his poetry and essays have concerned such work.

In 1970, Snyder built a house in the Sierra Nevada of Northern California, and he has lived at what he calls Kitkitdizze ever since. In 1990, Snyder and a group of his neighbors — people such as furniture maker Bob Erickson and carpenter Lenny Brackett — established the Yuba Watershed Institute, which its occasional journal Tree Rings describes as "a nonprofit organization...dedicated to discovery, research, and dissemination of information on the Yuba Watershed and to assisting in the management of the Inimim Forest."

At Kitkitdizze in the Yuba Watershed, Snyder carries on what he calls "the real work." This means knowing where your food and water come from so that you can actively participate in the decisions that affect the region in which you live; it requires hands-on work and living interdependently with the natural world. While Snyder teaches at the University of California at Davis and gives lectures and poetry readings to earn a wage, his aim is to avoid what he has called (in an interview with Peter Barry Chowkra in The Real Work) the "triple alienation" of contemporary life — alienation from energy and resources, the body, and the mind. This is why he is involved in all aspects of work at his home, why all members of his family are engaged in such work, why he has taught his daughter how to change the oil on the generators at Kitkitdizze, and why he has a deep love and respect for tools and knowing when to use the right tool. This is why, too, he respects men such as John Dofflemeyer, a California cattle rancher (and poet) working to maintain a traditional way of life on the land tempered with a sense of how to work in harmony with it.

Since the publication of his first book, Riprap, Snyder has explored these ideas in eight *collections of poetry, including* The Back Country, *the Pulitzer Prize-winning* Turtle Island, *and* No Nature: New and Selected Poems, *published last year. A collection of essays,* The Practice of the Wild, *addresses environmental and philosophical concerns.*

**Kevin Bezner:** How do you define the word "work," which in our culture seems to have taken on the definition of something you do to do something else?

**Gary Snyder:** You mean like "work" as occupation. That you have to do to support yourself. Yeah. That's actually called wage work, or wage earning, and as Ivan Illich points out in his very useful book called *Shadow Work*, working for wages is a very recent thing in history, and it's part of the rise of industrialism, the destruction of rural agriculture, and the creation of a working class. And in earlier times there's no work as defined in that way. One's life is one's subsistence is one's play is one's work. And it is not done in even a personal or individual way, it's done as part of what you do with your family and with other people, so that life is actually a family enterprise, or a household enterprise.

**KB:** That's what you have in your own life?

**GS:** Not entirely. Since we all live in a money economy, all of us in our household do some things that help bring money in. And some of what we do could be called wage earning. Some of what I do as a teacher at Davis could be wage earning, but the greater part of what I do could be called some kind of hunting and gathering. And as a writer it's very hard to draw the line between what's work, what's play, what's daily life in what you do in getting your material, seeing your world, being mindful, leading up to writing something. So that's more like the older sense that everything you do in life is done with an eye to subsistence. When you go for a walk, you watch for mushrooms. You come back with a couple of sticks of firewood. Is that work or is that play?

**KB:** One of your poems, that I admire the most is "The Bath." What you're doing there, in that poem, is the real work of showing your son Kai how one cleans oneself and how one lives in a family.

**GS:** Well, that's what you have to do with your kids no matter what. If you don't prove a leader to your own children and take time to show them each of the little things they have to do, and then take time out to help them learn to cook or help them learn to handle tools and involve them in the things that you do around the place, how are they ever going to learn? I'm teaching my little nine-year-old stepdaughter how to change the oil on the generator right now.

KB: How is she doing?

GS: She's perfect. If you take her through a procedure, she doesn't forget it. And she knows where the tools are. She's going to be dynamite when she's a little older. I'll have her fixing the cars.

KB: You have a family enterprise where you take people through the procedure, but you — and the people around you — seem to have moved into a way of taking the community through a procedure. In a sense, what you're doing with the Yuba Watershed Institute is showing people how they can live in the wild.

GS: What we're trying to do is learn how to do it ourselves first. In a sense, we're learning and showing at the same time. It's not exactly in the wilds, not in the wilds in the sense of protecting or preserved. It's primarily forest landscape — with some manzanita brush fields and a little bit of grazing and agricultural lands — in which we're all in the process of trying to learn to live and make some use of it, and at the same time enhance it. Some of that's public land, some of it's private land.

KB: Within this structure is a place for a Bob Erickson, who makes fine furniture and uses materials from the forest, and at the same time, there's a place for people who are attempting to preserve those forests.

GS: Bob does both himself. That's an example, it's one of the better examples that we have. Someone like Bob is able to make some use of the local hardwoods. And someone like Lenny Brackett, who is a fine carpenter and designs and builds traditional Japanese houses, is really tuned in to what's available locally. Like when it came to his attention that a very, very large old-growth sugar pine had died the next ridge over from a beetle kill, he was right over there on it and had it tagged by the Forest Service. He bought that dead tree and got it down on the ground and had that sawed up for lumber before the stain could get into it, because it was precious. In the lumber business as a whole, who's going to go out there for one snag? Lenny knew just what he wanted.

KB: The lumber business tends not to be local as well, and what you're talking about is a local economy.

GS: Right. That's very much part of it. The local economy can and will make it possible to precisely use one dead snag.

KB: How are we going to be able to find a way to bring out local economy values in a system that attempts to destroy or prevent that?

GS: It's extremely difficult. Obviously many people are not in a position to be able to even try. How do we keep family farms going? How do we keep a sustainable logging industry going that will be truly sustainable and at the same time make logging communities and logging culture viable? How do we have a sustainable ranching economy and ranching culture? Can the ranching culture have any place in the future? That's what John Dofflemeyer is working on. And maybe in a slightly larger picture is there any place for real skill, real craft in the working class at all, anywhere. Is there any place for a good carpenter? So much of our economy rewards you for being hasty and sloppy, and taking shortcuts, and even cheating. But it doesn't reward you for doing a good job. Or it only rewards you for doing a good job if you can sell your product to lawyers and doctors who will pay $3,000 for something unique. But not the economy at large.

KB: We're so rooted in a money economy that many people who have been exploited by companies and made dependent on an industry can't separate themselves out.

GS: We're seeing before our eyes right now the true face of this kind of capitalism. It talks a good line when it wants to, but when it's ready to pull out and move on and fire a bunch of people, it does it without a second thought. And what our current economic situation is doing — and maybe this isn't bad, maybe it's one of the good things — is that it's throwing people back on community and family resources. Young people in their twenties cannot afford often to rent a place on their own, an apartment or a house in the city. They come back and share in the family household, and families find themselves forced to try to make a family economy around the fact that they need more to live together; they need more to find ways to work together to make the family one of the bases of the economy. I see that happening more rather than less. And there's nothing shameful in that. It's only an American kind of vision of total fragmented independence, an individualism that gives people the idea that children should go away from home, everybody should live apart from each other, grandparents one place, aunts and uncles another place, children in another place. Yeah, we finally got the nuclear family. Whereas it's more normal and certainly more cost-effective to block out what we do together, like say the way an old Japanese farm family does. The slowing down of mobility in the United States, the fact that we have come to the limits of "boundless resources," and the fact that we are becoming more clearly aware that we need community as well as individual freedom — and that it's not impossible in some way to have the two together — is gradually making, as you would expect, American society slowly turn toward being more like a traditional society. There's good reason for it.

KB: By traditional, you mean?

GS: Larger families, family economies, the willingness to work together more. That becomes more of a possibility again now, I think, at least in some parts of American society. There are some parts that are alienated and fragmented, of course.

KB: So the conditions that are occurring now are prompting us to alter the larger view we have?

GS: Yeah. The older American view, which is the view of limitless resources, limitless opportunities, and "strike out on your own, young man, and go West," or whatever. That ceases to be a viable possibility. There's no West to strike out for. You can't afford an apartment in San Francisco, like I could in 1952. I came into San Francisco, got an entry-level laborer's job on the docks. With what I earned, I could afford to rent a small apartment on Telegraph Hill. A lot of younger people did that. Nobody can go to San Francisco, get an entry-level job, and afford to rent an apartment in the city any more.

KB: So much of this has to do with place, and making a commitment to place, and making a commitment to a community rather than the idea that we move about and shift places. Many in our culture, myself included, have moved where the work is.

GS: I appreciate that, certainly. I would like to say as a little caution against my own enthusiasms, though, that I don't think that "place" is automatically essential to this. It does happen more easily in place, but place can be a neighborhood in the city. It means just being someplace long enough to gets some roots down and do something together. So it's as important that neighborhoods and the green city movement make cities more livable. That's really critical. And I might add, just to go back a little bit, somebody might say to us, "Why, you guys are talking about family values." Well, yeah, we are talking about family values, and these are much more profound than the Republican Party's rhetoric, which simply refers to a few right-wing Christian moral principles and not to the idea about cooperation, or to the idea of community, of sharing. So when the Clinton campaign says the Republicans talk about family values but they don't do anything about it, it's right on.

KB: So we need to change our government as well?

GS: I would like to see the policies changed in corporations and in government hiring that require people to keep moving or they won't move up on the company ladder. There's built-in obligatory mobility in a lot of higher-level jobs in government and industry. Sometimes it makes some sense, a lot of the time it's probably not necessary. So that destroys a sense of place for such people. That keeps some of the most talented people from being rooted in any community.

KB: Do you think that if we approach a corporation with the right spirit and sensibility we can create a community there that will not negatively affect others within the larger community of our national culture?

GS: We have no choice but to try. Companies and corporate culture are here to stay, at least for quite some time. There are few companies that have tried out very creative, worthy practices. I'm thinking of Ben & Jerry's in Vermont that I understand is voluntarily paying the local dairy milk suppliers for their business a peg higher than the price standards set by the federal government; they recognize it cost the dairymen more than they would be paying them. They're voluntarily giving them more, and so they've made a choice to support their whole community economically. The Patagonia Corporation has incorporated child care and kindergartens right into the workplace, so that mothers bring their preschool children to work. Imagine a communitarian and somewhat more libertarian corporate culture. The next step is also to realize corporations can have a kind of culture, and they revel in it sometimes, but they lack place and they generally tend to bust place. They say, "Well, let's move this plant to Texas. All you guys go to Texas or you get docked." It would be incredible to see a corporation make a commitment to really stay in the place and become a part of the neighborhood. When we do that, we'll be beginning to make a big step towards healing America. I don't know many companies yet that have said, "We won't move from here." Truly bioregional companies. Although there might be some, I haven't heard of them.

KB: In summary, would you say the writer bears a specific responsibility, or any responsibility that goes beyond what the average citizen might have?

GS: Well, first of all, I would turn it the other way. Writers have the same responsibilities that other citizens have and they shouldn't forget it. In addition to that, they are the caretakers of the language and have a profound responsibility to tell the truth. Or the third Buddhist precept, "Do not abuse language." And that means a lot.

# happy man on welfare

*Today, the main temptations for violation of one's identity are the opportunities for advancement in industrial society.*
— Erich Fromm

*Zarathustra wants to be called a robber by the shepherds.*
— Nietzsche

*No, no, I am not without employment at this stage of the journey.*
— Henry Thoreau

Early in the spring. From the top tier of the Heywood Park grandstands, rush hour. There they go, in their armored vehicles, along the ruts of tradition. Lean efficiency is the rule of business out in high-tech corporation-land, but inefficiency rules the gridlock. Mostly single drivers: more empty seats than filled in that rat race. These drivers survived the last decade's "work" debacle, to form a kind of (nervous) working elite. The exscinded dross of *downsizing* and *rationalization* continues to multiply, dispersed through every community around the globe. Now "marginalized," now (sigh) "unemployed," now "giving up their dignity." *Outplaced*. No one will enslave them any more for a crumb of the pie, for the restaurant life, for the four-by-four and the big TV. No longer safe in the enframing, sterile halls, school corridors, bureaucratic cells.

Here comes the 1990s, and beyond that the tsunami of the Millennium. I am a literate tribal man in the extended margins. Parenthetical man, who cut through their ledger lines and escaped. It is a glorious Monday, says the sweep of my vision from the grandstands. There is unquestionable magic here — from here — about 8:30 A.M. in the morning of the year. In the sunshine they are building malls so that they can live inside a TV; sealed glass blocks, stores in a glaze-and-gloss consumer area. I am outdoors, building a sunshine weltanschauung from scratch and confusion.

I'm on welfare. Have been for a long time. I am in excellent physical shape (at forty), have a high IQ. I read much, am a freelance moralist, take full responsibility for my choice of income. I believe religiously that the world owes me a living.

Why, you lazy bastard! Parasite! Bum!

Yes indeed, I am lazy. I take that catchall catcall as a compliment. And a volunteer bastard. I didn't ask for official permission. Wilhelm Reich said, "Don't ask for a license to embrace your loved one." I would add: don't ask for a license to be born. Parasite? Of course. We all sit at another's table, animals, plants, included — all sit (or stand) at the earth's round table. That is nature's design in ecosystems. But...can you really "parasite" on an abundance? I must take issue with "bum" though. To me, "bum" evokes the image of a scruffy character "bumming" dimes or quarters. I have nothing against such people. But my family members, my friends, and you if we meet on the avenue, are safe from my solicitations. You gave at the office — I am grateful.

What to do with liberty on limited income? How to work one's leisure? Well, I liked Irving Layton's discovery late in life that all he wanted to do was "make love and make poems." I'll tell you about my love life another time. Also, in the freedom of many seasons, I followed Henry Thoreau's wise advice: "rise free from care before the dawn and seek adventures."

Why don't I get off my ass? In this society, childhood was twelve years of enforced discipline (conscript clientele of public schools). Periodically in "adulthood" I held "jobs." For what, friends? For who? For whose social system? For whose economy? For whose code of ethics? For whose bottom line? For whose topped-up bank account? For what preacher to preach — to preach what? For what teacher to teach — to teach what? For what "democracy"? For what "free" enterprise? For whose "world wars"? For whose "freedom"?

So I put my coat on and went outside. In the sun seasons, packed my daypack with thermos, mug, food, book to read (study), book to write in, felt-tipped pen, Walkman. I went mainly to the Heywood Park grandstands, Beacon Hill, A. J. Wood Bench, UVIC, Fleming Beach Heaths, the West Bay Boardwalk, scrubland paths beside the Selkirk Waters, the seawall below Ross Bay Cemetery, the Cemetery itself, the beaches along Dallas Road, Stadacona Park Rose Garden, and, when the opportunity arose, to deeper wilderness. By bicycle I sought philosophers' benches in the morning sun, and set to. Already off the bottom rung of their "ladder of success," their devil a-slide down the snakes (yahoo!). Already under the "bottom line" through which I had chopped a hole. Might as well take it further: dug down among the corpses. Communed with the ancestors.

The Road Not Taken runs over there, covered with underbrush, alder, protected by blackberry bushes. Way back that way it emerges from a very old tradition, the Western humanist and Christian, far older than the "work ethic" of the industrialists and their ideologues (Locke to Bentham) and their priests. It loops, makes an end run round suburban sprawls and urban enframings, and you can see it if you cock your eyes right, just about here. A tradition of aristocracies out of which came most of our treasury of "art," music, literature: the high dreams, aspirations of the race projected, modeled.

What makes this choice of aristocracy unique is that it is rooted as tenaciously as roadside weeds in the vision of democracy, and its path not taken: the dream of societies organized to nurture the development of individuals in their uniquenesses. This puts me at the top of the heap, as a free aristocrat, and off the bottom of the hierarchy, as not for sale.

Rush hour. Rush year, rush century. Like the tribesman who lay down after his first car ride to "let his soul catch up," I perch on the grandstands among crows and gulls in a light ecstasy and wait for mine.

Quieter after a time. Distant muted roar of the hives. The homeless are in town, I guess, I don't know where the rest of the unemployed are. A waft of fresh air tugs at my book.

I guess it was out of my own deep naiveté that I took the unacceptable road. How could I afford it? The most likely explanation was a moral deficiency. Somehow the delicately poised compass pointer of my social conscience had me tacking energetically against the zeitgeist.

I draw my knife. It turns out to be easy to cut that word, "work," from its main assumption, that which equates it with "job" (work that wants a boss to legitimize it, work that wants money to certify it).

Work                                                                      Job

OK. Well-separated. Word processing has revealed to me that the gap represented above is as wide or deep as you want. Put between the words a thousand miles of forests and rivers, or the child at work on her tree house. Second cut:

Leisure                                                                Laziness

Between these put Huck Finn's wide Mississippi. A hot summer day. Huck himself on a raft, barefoot, straw-hatted, lies back with his pipe and thinks what the blue sky thinks. "Laziness" and leisure are in love here, far from industry. And I am the thinking Huck. It is really the river that models archaic godlike laziness, so wide and leisurely it delivers the whole width of summer to the eye of the beholder. Withdraw from that bank an old dividend of leisure, a leisure ethic, that went under when the spirit of *industria* rose and bestrode the Western world.

What leisure ethic? Look to all of history's aristocrats, including Nature herself; the wild lion (endangered), yawning out on a high hot rock; old Pan himself, skirting the clear-cuts.

A man in his prime, bare-chested, oversees an empty baseball diamond and a stand of oaks. Rides the grandstands through the welcoming benignity of a new season. Feels an old and deep intelligence (*intelligere*: to choose between) shifting his tectonic plates. His soul!

I choose the free creative life. Not (this is crucial) fragments of "free time" in an overall context of indentured time. I wanted years in which to devote my "gifts," my talents, my enthusiasms, to projects that were not commanded by anybody but me and my own spirit's promptings.

A dreamer among the pragmatists: I wanted to gaze at the stars (*considere*, to observe the stars). Consider.

## TEN GOOD REASONS TO MAKE A NEW BID FOR FREEDOM IN THIS CENTURY:

1. R. Buckminster Fuller told the story of the 1955 meeting in Geneva of Soviet and American scientists to discuss possible peaceful uses of nuclear energy. Gerard Piel, publisher of *Scientific American*, was quoted there as saying that it was in scientific evidence that there could be not only enough of the living essentials to take care of everybody around the world at high standards of living, but that there also could be enough to take care of the increasing populations at ever-improving standards of living.

2. Tiny article in the *Victoria Times-Colonist* out of Geneva (May 22, 1986): The International Labor Organization announced after a study that the world will have to create 47 million new jobs every year for the next forty years…to overcome unemployment.

3. The *Times-Colonist* reported on January 12, 1988, that the world was spending $1.8 million a minute on armaments.

4. Today, says one source, there is the technological equivalent of 300 "energy slaves" per man, woman, and child.

5. From history we learn we are three or four lifetimes over our heads in a "work ethic" still dominant in media rhetoric, and a market ethos that is assumed. A "moralizing of the proletariat" initiated by the holders of economic power as the Industrial Revolution tooled up. They had a hell of a

time getting peasants and artisans into brutal factories out of their imme-
morial rhythms of seasons and the old way of long leisure and occasional
intense labor. A variety of unspeakable tortures impressed "duty" deeply
into children. Peaked in the nineteenth century. John Fowles: "Duty largely
consists of pretending that the trivial is critical."

6. The profit motive as we know it was conspicuously absent over most
of history. Unindustrialized people chose, if wages rose, not to work harder
but to take more time off. The Greeks didn't have a word for what we call
"work." Their word was *a-skolia*, "non-leisure," just as the Latin language had
*neg-otium*. *Skola*, meaning "leisure," is the root of our word for "school."

7. The idea of gain for gain's sake was foreign to Egyptian, Greek, Ro-
man, and medieval cultures, and mostly absent in the majority of Eastern
civilizations. In the Middle Ages the church taught that "no Christian
ought to be a merchant." Early capitalists were outcasts, bad guys. By 1700,
the turn had come. Check out the origins of Calvinism — a tragic path of
broken logic.

8. Family-systems psychology tells us that children "fantasy bond" to
abusive parents, defend them. Ergo, the "pride" of the worker in shameful
work. Beholden to the company. A refusal to support the idea of a guaranteed annual income ("jobs, not handouts"). Piven and Cloward, from their
book, *Regulating the Poor*: "When victims are induced to collaborate as vic-
timizers, submission is assured."

9. "Man as provider" came into Western collective consciousness in the
last century: to have a working wife meant that a man was less than a man.
Daniel Yankelovich did repeated surveys asking what was meant by a "real
man." Up to the late 1960s in the United States of America, a majority of
85 to 90 percent defined a "real man" as someone who is a "good provider."
In 1968 the number was 86 percent, but had fallen to 67 percent a decade
later. So the computer-age displaces, outplaces (liberates!) the robot's ser-
vant. What is left to them, though, poor devils, when the vessel of their
"manhood" is taken away? American mythos has a constant, ready answer:
violence. Violence, the other proof, certificate, of manhood.

10. The job, say Piven and Cloward is "the main institution by which
[people] are regulated and controlled."

Alvin Toffler says much the same in *Powershift*: "In the industrial world,
the paycheck became the basic tool of social control."

Control for what? you may inquire. To keep the rich rich (and growing
richer), the poor poor, and the invidious comparison between the two alive.
Why this setup and not something else? A dangerous question. What are the

sources of greed in a world of plenty? Material for an answer, heavy with schooling, "socialization," custom, culture, tips, and falls into the unconscious.

But Jung wrote, "Everything unconscious is projected."

Bertrand Russell said, "The morality of work is the morality of slaves," meaning the morality of the job. So did Nietzsche, who gave us the word *ressentiment*: the free-floating bitterness of the wage-slave and its tragic issue — "domestic violence," public violence, all the other familiar gross international by-products.

A couple of hours has passed, judging by the sun. A little woman walks by with her little dog. She doesn't look up at me. This beautiful open park is my living room, the grandstands my sun-blistered, green-painted easy chair. A line of trees, newly green, are elders assuming the post of educators in a class of one. Precious hours of *skola*. I lay down my book, try once more to "get" what the trees seem to be trying to convey, from their timeless Buddhistic equanimity.

"Man is the measure of all things." Am I not a member of that species? Social safety nets were originally spread out to prevent food riots, French Revolutions. The accelerating-acceleration curve of technological innovation climbs this century's walls, both here and in the rumbling giant called the developing world. "Externalized labor power" and "externalized rationale" multiplied a millionfold, dancing out and warring out humanity's great unconscious. And to the extent that we have suppressed or denied the implications of leisure, to that extent will its great projected god, Technology, wreak its revenge, its "thwarted love."

I measure all things.

There is a surplus base in this world. It is my experiment to plant my seed or nutshell of seeds in this surplus base. The house of survival: plenty for all. There it stands. The door is open — our house, the gift, the promise of the earth, its immanent physical principles. You do what you want. I'm going up to the summer fields. I'm going to follow up my interests, live out my hypothesis and my alluring long chances: scholarly, creative, erotic, ludic! I'm going to look out to sea, let my dreams drift down the sunsparkle trail. I'm going to consider a different face altogether of what is "important." I'm going out to play — over the whole earth!

JOE DOMINGUEZ AND VICHI ROBIN

# are you making a dying — or making a life?

Once upon a time "earning a living" was the means to an end: the means was earning, the end was living. But over time, earning a living has come to play a central role in our lives. For most working people, work for pay dominates their waking hours. Living is what can be fit into the remaining time. And despite it all, our savings are down and our debt is up. Is this really "earning a living," or is it more like "making a dying"?

But before "earning a living" there was work — it was part of daily life. Let's take a brief look at the history of work, for it is through history that we find opportunities to reshape our personal stories. Why do we work? And what is the place of work in our lives?

As human beings we all must do *some* work for basic survival — but how much? Is there a minimum daily requirement of work? A number of sources, ranging from primitive cultures to modern history, suggest that there is and would place this figure at about three hours a day during the adult lifetime.

Marshall Sahlins, author of *Stone Age Economics*, discovered that before Western influence changed daily life the !Kung bushmen of Botswana hunted from two to two-and-a-half days a week, with an average work

Adapted from *Your Money or Your Life*, by Joe Dominguez and Vicki Robin, copyright © 1992 by Viking.

week of fifteen hours. Women gathered food for about the same amount of time, and one day's work supplied each woman's family with vegetables for the next three days. Throughout the year both men and women worked for a couple of days then took a couple off to rest and play games, plan rituals, and enjoy each other's company. It would appear that the work-week in the old days beats today's bankers' hours by quite a bit!

Dr. Frithjof Bergmann, author of *Being Free*, corroborates this figure:

> For most of human history people only worked for two or three hours per day. As we moved from agriculture to industrialization, work hours increased, creating standards that label a person lazy if he or she doesn't work a forty hour week... The very notion that everyone should have a job only began with the Industrial Revolution.

In his study of utopian communities of the nineteenth century, John Humphrey Noyes, founder of Oneida community, noted that:

> All these communities have demonstrated what the practical Dr. Franklin (of the 18th century) said, that if every one worked bodily three hours daily, there would be no necessity of any one's working more than three hours.

These studies suggest that three hours a day is all that we *must* spend working for survival. One can imagine that, in preindustrial times, this pattern would make sense. Life was more of a piece back then when work blended into family time, religious celebrations, and play. Then came the "labor-saving" Industrial Revolution and the compartmentalization of life into work and nonwork, with work taking an ever-bigger bite out of the average person's day. By the turn of the century the workweek was up to sixty hours — a far cry from the three hours a day of our ancestors.

In the late nineteenth century the "common man," with justified aversion to such long hours on the job, began to fight for a shorter workweek. Champions for the workers claimed that fewer hours on the job would decrease fatigue and increase productivity. Indeed, they said, fewer hours was the natural expression of the maturing Industrial Revolution; it would free the workers to exercise their higher faculties and democracy would enjoy the benefit of an educated and engaged citizenry.

But all that came to a halt during the Depression. The workweek, having fallen dramatically to thirty-five hours, became locked in at forty hours for many and has even crept up to fifty or even sixty hours a week in the last two decades.

Why? During the Depression, free time became equated with unemployment. In an effort to boost the economy and reduce unemployment, the New Deal established the forty-hour workweek, and the government became the employer of last resort. Workers were educated to consider employment, not free time, to be their right as citizens. Benjamin Kline Hunnicutt, in *Work Without End*, points out:

> Since the Depression, few Americans have thought of work reduction as a natural, continuous, and positive result of economic growth and increased productivity. Instead, additional leisure has been seen as a drain on the economy, a liability on wages, and the abandonment of economic progress.

For the last half-century this has translated as a push for full employment, and leisure has been translated into a commodity to be consumed rather than free time to be enjoyed. This has meant more people with more "disposable income," which meant increased profits, which meant business expansion, which meant more jobs, which meant more consumers with yet more disposable income. Consumption has kept the wheels of progress moving.

Our concept of leisure has changed radically. From a desirable and civilizing component of day-to-day life, leisure has become idleness, a reminder of the painful unemployment during the Depression years. As the value of leisure has dropped, the value of work has risen. The push for full employment, along with the growth of advertising, has created a populace increasingly oriented toward work and toward earning more money in order to consume more resources.

In addition, during the last half-century the fabric of family, culture, and community that gave meaning to life outside the workplace has begun to unravel. The traditional rituals, the socializing, and the simple pleasure of one another's company all provided structure for nonwork time, affording people a sense of purpose and belonging. Without this experience of being part of a people and a place, leisure leads more often to loneliness and boredom.

Because life outside the workplace has lost vitality and meaning, work ceases being a means and becomes an end in itself. Jobs now serve the function that traditionally belonged to religion: they are where we seek answers to the perennial questions of "Who am I?" and "Why am I here?" and "What's it all for?"

Jobs are called upon to provide the exhilaration of romance and the depths of love. It's as though we believed that there is a Job Charming out there — like the Prince Charming in fairy tales — that will fill our needs and inspire us to greatness. We've come to believe we would somehow have it all through our job: status, meaning, adventure, luxury, respect, power, tough challenges, and fantastic rewards! Perhaps what keeps some of us stuck in the home-workplace loop is this very Job Charming illusion. Like the princess who keeps kissing toads looking for a handsome prince, we keep changing jobs looking for our personal fulfillment.

Perhaps most detrimentally, we look to our jobs to provide us with a sense of identity. Remember the question we were asked in childhood: "What do you want to be when you grow up?" Do you remember what you answered? Are your teen-age dreams tucked away with your high-school yearbook? Has your job history bumped and turned on byways you would never have predicted on "Career Day" in high school? If you went on to "be what you wanted to be," has it met your expectations?

The very question, "What do you want to *be* when you grow up?" reveals the problem. It asks what you want to "be," yet you are supposed to answer it with a "do." Is it any wonder that so many of us suffer midlife crises as we face the fact that our "doing" doesn't even come close to expressing our "being"?

We are so wedded to what we do that we perpetuate, without thinking, this confusion of doing with being. We've come to take our sense of self from our jobs, and even our closest relationships take a back seat. Indeed, in terms of sheer hours, we may be more wedded to our jobs than to our mates.

This confusion of job and identity puts us in a bind. For example, we notice that, thanks to our increasing worship of working and spending, we Americans have the lowest savings rate in the industrial world and the highest per capita debt in our history. Certainly getting out of debt and accumulating savings would give us independence and freedom to choose, reduce our reliance on paid employment, and allow unemployment to be a golden opportunity for discovery, learning, and renewal. But what if you think that who you *are* is what you *do* to make money? No amount of savings would save you from that loss of purpose and self-esteem. Who you are is far greater than what you do for money, and your true work is far greater than your paid employment. Our focus on money and materialism may have robbed us of the pride we can and should feel in who we are as people and the many ways we contribute to the well-being of others. Our task now is to retrieve that birthright of knowing ourselves as human *beings* rather than human *doings* or human *earnings*.

Perhaps it is time to redefine work, and in so doing distinguish between paid employment and true work. Paid employment has one purpose — getting paid. Work, on the other hand, is activity that expresses your values and dreams and fulfills your sense of meaning and purpose in life.

Our ancestors, with their three-hour workdays, remind us that earning a living does not have to take our whole life. There are other options; options like working part-time, be it working two days a week or four months a year or job-sharing — or even consolidating our wage-earning, working intensively for a limited and finite period of time to earn enough money to take care of our needs for the rest of our lives. Time liberated from the *necessity* of working for a living allows us to devote ourselves to the things that give life real meaning — family, increased creativity, and development of one's unique contribution. By limiting our addictive acquisitiveness, reducing our needs, and learning to live more frugally, earning a living can once again take its place as a means to the end of a whole and fulfilling life.

Author's notes: References and quotations are derived from *Stone Age Economics* by Marshall Sahlins (Chicago: Aldine-Atherton, 1972); Frithjof Bergmann, author of *Being Free* (University of Notre Dame Press, 1977), in *Green Light News*, Vol. 1, No. 1, 1984; *The History of American Socialism* by John Humphrey Noyes (Philadelphia: Lippincott, 1870); and *Working Without End* by Benjamin Kline Hunnicutt (Philadelphia: Temple University Press, 1988).

# credits

## Sherman Alexie

Sherman Alexie, a Spokane/Coeur d'Alene Indian, is a full time writer. He has published three books of poetry and short stories, including *The Business of Fancydancing*, *I Would Steal Horses*, and *Old Shirts & New Skins*. Atlantic Monthly Press will be publishing his collection of short stories, *The Lone Ranger Fist Fight in Heaven*, and a novel, *Coyote Springs*. Sherman says his two worst jobs were washing dishes in the student union center on twelve-hour shifts and delivering pizzas. However, he made more money on the pizza job than on any other since.

## James H. Barker

"For most of my adult life I've been a photographer. In 1974 I moved to Bethel, Alaska, to begin the ethnographic documentation of Yup'ik Eskimos. The book, *Always Getting Ready*, includes photographs dating from 1973 to 1992. I prefer selecting situations to document that allow plenty of time to delve into the subtleties of people's lives. The longer time I spend the more I feel like a participant than an observer. This length of time also allows me to study the results and keep shooting until the photographs accumulated seem to replicate the impressions that I've gained."

## Greg Bear

Greg Bear is an author of science fiction and fantasy. He is married to Astrid Anderson Bear and is the father of two, Erik and Alexandra. He has published more than sixteen books and been the recipient of major awards, including a Nebula, a Hugo, and the Prix Apollo.

## Stephen J. Beard

Stephen J. Beard has worked as a laborer, mailman, used-car salesman, newspaper reporter, snack-foods distributor, vending-machine mechanic, auto mechanic, editor of a singles magazine, public relations manager, corporate communications executive and manager of an international trade association. Holding these jobs, he was hired, fired, and laid off more times than he cares to recall. Steve works nowadays as a business journalist, a technical writer, and editor. He is also associate editor of *Left Bank*, but he refuses to consider that job or any of the others he performs to earn his money as having anything to do with his identity.

146

## Kevin Bezner

Kevin Bezner is a freelance writer in Missoula, Montana. His interviews have appeared in a variety of publications, including *American Poetry Review*, *Denver Quarterly*, *Mississippi Review*, and *Sonora Review*.

## Kate Braid

Kate Braid has written prose and poetry about her fifteen years as a carpenter, building houses, high-rises and bridges. For a complete change of pace she is now director of the Labour Program at Simon Fraser University in British Columbia. Her book, *Covering Rough Ground* (Polestar Press) won the Lowther Award for best book by a Canadian woman poet in 1991.

## Kent Chadwick

Kent Chadwick has tended barrels for a California winery, taught English to junior high school kids in Newark and university students in Osaka, waited tables in Pullman, Washington, and edited the *Northwest Ethnic News* in Seattle. His poetry has appeared in *Sojourners* and the anthology *Deep Down Things: Poems of the Inland Pacific Northwest*.

## Robin Cody

A graduate of Yale, Robin Cody taught at the American School of Paris and was dean of admissions at Reed College in Portland before taking up freelance writing in 1983. *Ricochet River*, published by Alfred A. Knopf in 1992, is his first novel. He is currently working for Knopf on a nonfiction book about a canoe trip down the Columbia River, from source to mouth. While writing, he moonlights as a baseball umpire and a basketball referee.

## Joe Dominguez and Vicki Robin

Having followed their own good advice, Joe Dominguez and Vicki Robin live high on the hog but low on the economic scale in Seattle, Washington. Their frugality provides them the freedom to devote their time to friends and to the

New Road Map Foundation, a nonprofit educational and charitable organization designed to provide tools for personal empowerment to people who want to serve more than their little local selves. Joe and Vicki wrote the best-selling *Your Money or Your Life* (Viking, 1992) to share their nine-step program to financial freedom with those millions of Americans who are beginning to wake up from the dream and search for a practical approach to money, and life.

147

## Tom Harpole

"I've written and read my essays on subjects from bull riding to dynamiting on Ireland's Radio Eirann, and America's National Public Radio. My most recent nonfiction pieces on skydiving with Soviet paratroopers and the Russian space program appeared in Smithsonian's magazine, *Air & Space*. I am still a licensed blaster shooting stumps, ditching swamps, cracking rock and foundations, beaver dams and ice jams. Out of high school I began finding compelling work: in 1967 I got a job with some winning funny car drag racers. I was lifeguard at the rooftop pool of the Denver Playboy club during summers between college."

## Robert Heilman

Robert Heilman planted about 150,000 trees during five winter planting seasons. "Overstory: Zero" is from his book of essays, *Manual Labor (and other things not taught in schools)*, a seven-year labor of love that is nearing completion. A columnist, freelance writer, and storyteller, he lives with his wife and son in Myrtle Creek, Oregon.

## Sibyl James

Sibyl James's most recent books are *In China with Harpo and Karl* (Calyx Books) and *The Adventures of Stout Mama* (Papier-Mache). She is currently working on a book about her experiences as a Fulbright professor in Tunisia. "My résumé looks unstable," she says, "because it lists so many different employers, but it really reflects the insecure employment situation faced by so many college teachers. As my friend Ed Harkness said when we were both preparing to teach in China, 'For the first time in our lives, we're being offered a one-year contract with medical benefits.'"

## William Johnson

Bill Johnson teaches literature and writing at Lewis-Clark State College in Lewiston, Idaho. He has written *What Thoreau Said* (University of Idaho Press, 1991) and is completing a manuscript of poems entitled *The Task*. He has worked as a potato-mucker, carpenter's assistant, railroad crew-caller, janitor, and general flunky in a frozen-food processing plant. Teaching is a lark, he says, but he relishes working with his hands. Favorite tools: garden fork, fly rod, guitar.

## Norman Maclean

Norman Maclean's first book, *A River Runs Through It and Other Stories*, was published when he was seventy-three. He died in 1990 and his final book, *Young Men and Fire*, was published to great acclaim in 1992. The book, a project that completely occupied Maclean's final years, was based on the 1949 Mann Gulch fire that resulted in the tragic deaths of most of the members of the Forest Service's elite crew of firefighters.

## Adrian Raeside

Adrian Raeside, originally from New Zealand, is a cartoonist for the Victoria, British Columbia, *Times-Colonist*. He is syndicated in seventy newspapers in Canada and appears in American and international publications, including some in Russia and Japan. His new Sunday comic strip, "Toulose," is now in syndication in the U.S. and Canada. Adrian's animated cartoons have been seen on "Sesame Street" and used by Turner Broadcasting. Sono Nis Press published his book of political humor, *Five Twisted Years: B.C. — What Really Happened.*

## Jack Saturday

Jack Saturday is the pseudonym of a Vancouver, British Columbia, writer.

## Joan Skogan

Joan Skogan wrote the children's books *Grey Cat at Sea* and *The Princess and the Sea Bear and Other Tsimshian Stories* (both with Polestar Press) and an oral history called *Skeena: A River Remembered*. She has spent plenty of time on boats and the last six years as a foreign fishery observer offshore.

## Toby Sonneman

Toby Sonneman was a migrant worker for fifteen years. Now an independent writer, artist, and activist for Romani rights, she lives with her husband, photographer Rick Steigmeyer, and their two children in the orchard country of Cashmere, Washington.

## Clem Starck

Clem Starck has earned a living by various means, some less onerous than others. At one time or another he has worked as a paperboy, a soda jerk, a dishwasher, a waiter, a construction laborer, a gandy dancer, a cowboy, a rigger, a newspaper reporter, a proofreader, a carpenter, a merchant seaman, a door-to-door salesman, a general contractor, a carpenter foreman, a construction superintendent, a building dismantler, and a college professor, but mostly as a carpenter and carpenter foreman, building anything from cabinets to bridges. At present he is gainfully employed by Oregon State University in Corvallis as a carpenter. A collection of his poems, *Journeyman's Wages*, is due out later this year from Story Line Press.

## Richard Stine

Richard Stine's "autobiodyssey" began in 1940, and soon there were memories "of making art — gluing, drawing, working in clay, wood, metal. Everyone in our family made things....After the 6th grade, except for free play, I hated school....in high school my art teacher saved me from the system....When my interest in college ground to a halt,...I headed for Europe, lived on various Greek islands, in Paris, in London, cruised on ships here and there and around the world, returned to America, punched cattle, made burgers, drove trucks, moved furniture, sold toys, worked for Linus Pauling, worked at Hearst Castle, got married, had a son, moved to Santa Barbara, California and at twenty-eight, finally started to make some money from my art. ¶From Santa Barbara...to Ojai, California,...where a patron offered me room and board in exchange for my art. And for the next twenty years, even after the patron was long gone, I made things — mostly drawings, in a studio above a hardware store that looked out over a parking lot up into the mountains and into the sky. Most of these drawings were published in the *Los Angeles Herald Examiner* and *The San Francisco Chronicle* regularly for many years. They are still published and distributed internationally in books, on posters, on T-shirts and on greeting cards. ¶Early in 1989 I moved...to an island off Seattle, where I've lived with my wife and clever black dog ever since. ¶Along the way, we started a publishing company (Pal Press)...The income from this keeps us going. ¶I don't know if I ever became an artist in the way other artists become artists. I never got a B.A., M.A., M.F.A. or a Pee-H-Dee. I've never received a grant and never been published in *The New Yorker*, though many people insist I have.

## John Strawn

John Strawn has been a teacher, a carpenter, and a general contractor, but his oddest job was microfilming the personal papers of the design guru Buckminster Fuller. Strawn's last book, *Driving the Green*, is now a HarperPerennial paperback. His next book, from Nan Talese/Doubleday, an account of a plant-hunting expedition to Chilean Patagonia, is due in 1994.

## Jeff Taylor

A former contributing editor of *New Age Journal* and *Mother Earth News*, humorist Jeff Taylor now writes regular essay columns for *Harrowsmith* (Canada) and *GreenPrints* as well as a short story for every issue of *BackHome*. He has lectured on writing humor at the sybaritic and Byzantine Aspen Writer's Conference. A life-long carpenter and blue-collar churl, he enjoyed two strange years as a technical writer and corporate lackey for a giant homebuilding corporation, whose lifestyle duties included driving a BMW and sucking down Dove Bars and sushi. It was apparently a linchpin job; the entire conglomerate went into receivership just after he left.

150

## Kyle Walker

Kyle Walker is a freelance writer based in Seattle.

## Tom Wayman

Tom Wayman divides his time between his duties as the Squire of "Appledore," an estate in the Selkirk Mountains near Nelson, British Columbia, and as a professor of English and creative writing for Okanagan University College in Vernon and Kelowna, British Columbia. Two of his books are *Inside Job: Esssays on the New Work Writing* (1983) and *Paperwork*, an anthology of contemporary United States and Canadian poems about employment (1991), both from Harbour Publishing. House of Anansi Press published in June of 1993 a new collection of Wayman's essays, entitled *A Country Not Considered: Canada, Culture, Work*. Wayman's work experience includes construction, demolition, and factory work. He was a founding member (1979) of the Vancouver Industrial Writers Union, a work-based writers circle still functioning.

## Teri Zipf

Teri Zipf halfheartedly denies any resemblance between herself and the former Mrs. Kosiki. She has, however, been published and rejected by many of the same places as her fictional creation. In 1992 she received a Fishtrap fellowship. She is currently a senior in English at Walla Walla College and will begin teaching college writing and poetry later this year.

*W*e two sisters are nearing the end of our second year of publishing *Glimmer Train Stories*. Each quarterly issue offers up our favorite dozen short stories out of the three thousand or so we receive every submission month. They make for a stirring and luxurious read:

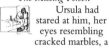

JOYCE CAROL OATES
*The Missing Person*

Ursula had stared at him, her eyes resembling cracked marbles, a tawny light-fractured sheen, unnervingly beautiful, as in a moment of extreme intimacy.

RICHARD BAUSCH
*The Natural Effects of Divorce*

"Every marriage," his mother said, sniffling, "is like a covered dish. There's no guessing what really goes on."

STEPHEN DIXON
*Interstate 3, Paragraph 2*

And he shouts, "Oh no, what're we going to do? Keep down, down," and they're screaming and he thinks, Think, come on, what should you do? Oh my poor children.

Each issue also includes a column by Siobhan Dowd, director of PEN's Freedom-to-Write, and two interviews with writers and other artists.

Doris Lessing:
*Voice of England, Voice of Africa*
Interview by MICHAEL UPCHURCH

I'm not interested in politics. Wait, that's not true. I'm *fascinated* by politics. But I don't believe anymore in these great, rhetorical causes. I'm much more interested in smaller, practical aims: things that can be done.

Unlike other short-story magazines, *Glimmer Train* is ad-free, but more importantly:

It is their keen and revealing sensitivity which distinguishes these stories; it is their insightfulness into characters and situations which marks their creativity.
—*The Small Press Book Review*

A handsome paperback, printed on acid-free, recycled paper, *Glimmer Train* is also visually satisfying:

The format features a glorious color cover, numerous black and white illustrations, and unique author photos. Most magazines of such quality and imagination wither and die within a few issues. Let's hope this does not happen to *Glimmer Train*.
—*W.P. Kinsella*

[Editors' note: Thankfully, sales have doubled our print-run since issue one.]

Every story is illustrated by a fine hand and is prefaced with an author profile including her or his childhood photograph and personal caption. Know who this is?

*(Kiran Kaur Saini, poet and author of "A Girl Like Elsie.")*

We're happy to report that other people seem to like *Glimmer Train* as much as we like putting it together:

The stories…are among the best I've read in years and there are lots of them, presented with style. Open the magazine and you're drawn in hard. *Glimmer Train* won't let you go until the last story is told.
—*Laughing Bear Newsletter*

I love *Glimmer Train*. No pretension—everything goes to the bone.
—*Anne Chacon*

*For $29 a year, each quarter we'll send you 160 pages full of great short stories—a feast of fiction.*

The stories individually and the magazine collectively are absolutely first-rate… Excellent artwork, too. A bargain, by God, a bargain.—*Eric Rush*

Please mail or fax your Visa/MC number and expiration date, or send your $29 check to:
**Glimmer Train Press, Inc.**
812 SW Washington Street
Suite 1205
Portland, OR 97205
FAX: 503/221-0837
**Attention writers:**
Send SASE for guidelines.

# LEFT BANK

## A new way to read between the lines — a potlatch of pointed prose and poetry.

Semiannual in December & June, **LEFT BANK** is a book series featuring NW writers on universal themes. Readers are treated to a provocative, entertaining, and evocative cross-section of creative nonfiction, fiction, essays, interviews, poetry, and art.

Themes are determined by an editorial staff and advisory board of respected writers, editors, and publishers from Alaska, British Columbia, Idaho, Montana, Oregon, and Washington.

*#1: Writing & Fishing the Northwest* — features the likes of Wallace Stegner, Craig Lesley, Sharon Doubiago, Greg Bear, Nancy Lord, and John Keeble.

*#2: Extinction* — read it before it disappears. David Suzuki introduces Barry Lopez, David Quammen, Tess Gallagher, Sallie Tisdale, Robert Michael Pyle, John Callahan, Nancy Lord, and others.

*#3: Sex, Family, Tribe* — get intimate with Ursula K. Le Guin, William Stafford, Ken Kesey, Colleen McElroy, William Kittredge, Charles Johnson, and Matt Groening.

*#4: Gotta Earn a Living* — you've got it.

*#5: Border & Boundaries* — go to the edge with Michael Dorris, Sandra Scofield, Robert Sheckley, and others.

BOOKSTORES, ORDER FROM YOUR FAVORITE WHOLESALER OR FROM: Consortium Book Sales & Distribution, 1045 Westgate Drive, St. Paul, Minnesota 55114-1065.

REQUEST OUR CATALOG. AND ASK FOR WRITERS' GUIDELINES — YOU JUST NEVER KNOW.

# LEFT BANK

— a great gift to give yourself or any thoughtful friend who enjoys the adventure of superb writing. Just photocopy this page, fill in the form below, and send it today. Subscriptions are $14, postage paid, and begin with the next issue/edition to be published, but back issues are available for $7.95 plus $2 shipping and handling.

Send **LEFT BANK** to me at:

Send a gift subscription to:

I'd like the following back issues:

My order total is:

I've enclosed a check or Money Order — or charge my VISA or MC; its number and expiration are: